Three Tales

GUSTAVE FLAUBERT

THREE TALES

Translated by Arthur McDowall

Introduction by Harry Levin

Published by New Directions

THE NEW CLASSICS

Norfolk, Connecticut · Mcmxliv

MANUFACTURED IN THE UNITED STATES OF AMERICA
BY THE VAIL-BALLOU PRESS, INC., BINGHAMTON, N. Y.

CONTENTS

Introduction

To SAY that these stories contain Flaubert's maturest writing is as much as can be said for any prose. Flaubert himself said he would rather die like a dog than force out an immature phrase. His frequently revised drafts and his sharply self-critical letters corroborate him, and show us something of the years and pains that maturity cost him. His spiritual autobiography, *L'Éducation sentimentale,* estimates the price his generation paid in terms of political disillusionment. The last decade of his life, beginning with the fall of France in 1870, continued with the grudging reception of his most meditated book, *La Tentation de Saint-Antoine,* and with the failure of his political satire, *Le Candidat,* on the stage. His mother's death deprived him of his sole companion, and he sold his property to stave off the bankruptcy of his niece's husband. His mental and physical health, never certain, was worse than ever. His work in progress, *Bouvard et Pécuchet,* was hardly a consolation. Deso-

lation was the keynote of all his novels, wrote
George Sand, one of his few surviving friends.
To console himself, in 1875, he turned from his
monumental survey of modern follies to a series
of miniatures.   First, rather tentatively, to *La
Légende de Saint-Julien l'hospitalier;* then to
Un Cœur simple, the legend of a modern saint;
but George Sand, who died in 1876, had no
chance to read the masterpiece inspired by her
advice.   In 1877 *Hérodias* was written and
Trois contes was published.   Completed in
eighteen months, it was the last book that Flaubert completed, and the book that brought him
closest to his critics and to the public.

The history of civilization, by Flaubert's mor-
dant reckoning, was divided into three periods:
paganism, Christianity, and—the names he reserved for the bourgeoisie are sometimes un-
translatable—*muflisme*.   From each of these
periods he chose a protagonist whom he cele-
brated at full length: *Salammbô, Saint-Antoine,*
and *Madame Bovary*.   Repeating the pattern
on a small scale, he chose a less desolating trio.
Even the pagan sinner, Herodias, was over-
shadowed by the Christian saint, John the
Baptist.   Anthony too had been a saint, but his
ordeal had been Flaubert's conception of the
anchoritic life of the artist; whereas Julian found

salvation in "the need to mingle with the lives of others," in the service of his fellow men, in a fraternal embrace. As for the simple heart, her story was submerged in other lives, and Flaubert delicately extricated it. It was a sequel to *Madame Bovary,* more particularly to the episode at the agricultural show, where Cathérine Leroux, a single heroic figure in a crowd of *mufles,* had been cited for half a century of servitude. Félicité—the most real of Flaubert's heroines and one of his few men or women of good will—sprang from the same peasant stock, belonged to the same Norman countryside, and incarnated the same "animal-like devotion and religious veneration." Flaubert knew how it felt to be stricken down in a winter night on the road between Pont-l'Évêque and Honfleur; for there the nervous crisis had taken place that determined his career, leading him to abandon Paris and the law for Croisset and his art. An intense bond of personal sympathy drew him to Félicité, as to another victim of the coachman's whip, the blind man who dogged the errant footsteps of Emma Bovary.

Flaubert is commonly regarded as an impersonal and unsympathetic writer, yet his work is rich in positive values, which appear most concretely when he touches his native soil. In

search of material for "A Simple Heart" he
revisited Trouville, where he and his sister had
spent idyllic summers, like Paul and Virginie.
Overcome by an almost Proustian nostalgia, he
sank—as he told his correspondents—into "a
bath of recollections." The farm, the inn, the
townspeople, the relatives, and the servant were
part of his own recovered past. When his imagination ranged into more remote provinces,
with the pilgrimage of Saint Julian, it returned
to a stained-glass window in the Rouen Cathedral. It may indeed have started from a sculp-
tured relief over one of the portals, in pursu-
ing the exotic narrative of Saint John's death.
Statues of the Last Judgment and the Damned
in Hellfire—readers of *Madame Bovary* will
not forget—looked down reprovingly on Emma
and Léon, as their curtained fiacre took the road
to the country. Flaubert's landscapes are dis-
cernible in the paintings of Courbet or the Bar-
bizon school, but they were never as naïvely
literal as the new realism of the painters. Com-
pare the faded attractions of Gustave Moreau's
Danse de Salomé, which captivated the Salon of
1876, with the opening paragraphs of "Herodias." If there is any parallel for the plastic
qualities of Flaubert's imagery, it is the newer
impressionism: the economy of means, the unity

of tone, the contrasting color, and the ubiquitous mist.   Here again, as he often said, his books exhale the misty atmosphere of Normandy. They lure us, after Julian, into "countries where there are so many mists that we are surrounded by phantoms."

Despite his Norman hard-headedness, there was an irrepressible element of fantasy in Flaubert, to which he gave free rein in "The Legend of Saint Julian."   Thomas Mann might call this story a *Romanteppich,* for it has the plasticity of a fine tapestry, and its texture—like the heavier texture of Mann's Joseph story—is based on an age-old configuration of sin and sacrifice.   If "The Ancient Mariner" has a moral, so has Julian's adventure : wilful cruelty to animals is duly avenged by nature.   But Flaubert's nature is more like Vigny's than Coleridge's, more ironic than sympathetic.   The stoical suffering of beasts is always a touchstone, a source of tragic dignity in a naturalistic world, and a peculiar horror lurks behind the esthetic sadism of the hunt and the parricide. Hounded by guilt and anxiety, monstrous phantoms yet strangely familiar, we stray toward the dream-world of Freud and Kafka : "everything happening with the ease that we experience in dreams."   In the greyish daylight of provincial routine, things do not happen so easily; the saint's life, however, still serves as the genre for Félicité's biography—not ironically, Flaubert insisted, but seriously and sadly.   Miracles are reduced to articles of religious belief, ritual provides the color that would otherwise be lacking, and the stuffed parrot finally attains a niche in Flaubert's Gothic iconography.   Its transfiguration reveals the Holy Ghost, just as Julian's leper revealed Christ.   Victor Hugo's formula for romantic art, the juxtaposition of the grotesque and the sublime, is satisfied.   But "A Simple Heart" solves—as Dostoevsky and few others have done—a more difficult problem: it reveals the sublime in the grotesque.

quote

Background, if not temperament, made Flaubert a realist.   Clinical touches throughout his work remind us that he had grown up in a hospital.   Notes on Biblical exegesis, medieval falconry, and the habits and diseases of psittacids documented the composition of *Three Tales*. "Monotony of their existence—little facts," he noted, in a preliminary sketch of Mme. Aubain's household.   The problem of filling in the sketch was to describe the monotony without becoming monotonous, to endow the little facts with subjective significance.   Balzac and the other realists had garnered detail for detail's sake, but

Flaubert included no detail that did not have an idea behind it, no physical fact that did not help to establish a psychological mood. Consider his description of Félicité's room, an authentic shrine of family relics, each of them hallowed by some personal association. Objects are transmuted into symbols. Their significance lies not in objective reality, but in their powers of evocation. A worn plush hat evokes the dead Virginie; the inventory of her wardrobe is a link of poignant equality between Félicité and Mme. Aubain. Loulou becomes a fetish, linked to Félicité's existence through memories of her sea-faring nephew, and immolated on one of those Corpus Christi altars that she and Virginie had decorated together. The ultimate ceremony, her deathbed scene, should be contrasted with the famous chapter in which Emma Bovary receives extreme unction; the same associative technique is used, but it summons up different associations, which emphasize the difference between two ways of life. Thus Flaubert, at his maturest, anticipates the symbolic method and thematic structure of Proust, and encourages further explorations into the stream of consciousness.

Flaubert is better known, perhaps, for his technique of dissociation. Again we recall the

agricultural show in *Madame Bovary,* where
the orator's banalities undercut the lover's advances.   An equally brilliant passage of coun-
terpoint occurs at the banquet in "Herodias,"
where a theological disputation is seasoned by
the names of luxurious dishes.   The last word
in the story, the eloquent adverb *alternative-
ment,* is a kind of signature.   But Flaubert's
irony—unlike that of his facile imitator, Anatole
France, in *Le Procurateur de Judée*—is on the
side of Christianity, and against the spiritual
obtuseness of Pharisees and publicans.   Without relaxing his lifelong skepticism, he shared
Renan's admiration for the historical role of "a
certain Jesus," for the incorruptibility of the
saints and the fathers, and for the richness of
Catholic culture.   This is the central conception
that integrates his three tales.   Having suggested that a simple life in Normandy need not
be spiritually impoverished, he went on to sug-
gest the provinciality of life *à la Bas-Empire.*
His immediate preoccupation was not religion, he said, so much as "the question of
races"; apart from "the savage expression of
Herodias," he was fascinated by "the official
countenance of Herod (who was a true pre-
fect)."   The situation defined itself politically:
a proud citadel, flying its eagles over Galilee,

the outpost of a corrupt imperialism; a voice out of the depths, prophesying ruin and exile, expecting liberation with the advent of the Messiah; an uneasy Tetrarch, caught between the proconsul and the prophet, intriguing Romans and wrangling Jews. Where the first two tales have been biographical, the third approaches the dramatic form, and its third act approaches a theatrical climax.

Salome's dance, though it untangles the denouement, is hardly more than a stroke of policy on the part of Herodias. It gives us a brief glimpse of Kuchouk Hanem, the Egyptian dancer who also posed for Salammbô, but it does not go far beyond the stark outlines of Matthew (XIV, 1–12) or Mark (VI, 17–19). It remained for Mallarmé and Huysmans to bring out the decadent eroticism of this theme, and for Oscar Wilde, Aubrey Beardsley, and Richard Strauss to plot the choreography of a *fin-de-siècle* strip-tease. As a stimulus to other writers, the effects of Flaubert's slight volume are still being registered; they have been extended to contemporary American writing through *Three Lives,* the most successful of Gertrude Stein's attempts to let the inarticulate speak for itself. *Three Tales,* looking back in the other direction to the gospels and the Golden

Legend, epitomizes the whole cycle of fiction. Romanticism and realism, naturalism and symbolism—all those tendencies, which conflict in theory, are resolved in practice. If "A Simple Heart" exploits a realistic vein, "The Legend of Saint Julian" escapes to an ideal realm, while "Herodias" justifies Hugo's comment that Flaubert combined "the real, which exhibits life, with the ideal, which reveals the soul." On a more practical plane, he contributed largely to the development of the short story, to the peculiarly French tradition that he inherited from Mérimée and passed on to Maupassant. Too much attention has been concentrated on his phrasing, and not enough on his technical innovations. Some of his devices are as old as the art of narrative; others—varying modes of presentation, unexpected angles of observation—are as modern as the film. As examples of craftsmanship, they can be studied with greater profit than the machine-made imitations that his pupils are now producing.

Flaubert's credo, since it recognizes no substitute for the unique phrase, discourages translators. It is fortunate, therefore, that Mr. McDowall has persisted, and the present endeavor to place his translation before a wider public needs no apology. Following his English version from the French text has increased my appreciation of the many difficulties involved, and of his skill in surmounting them.   A few of them, unfortunately, are insurmountable. Rhythm must necessarily yield to meaning—a circumstance that Flaubert used to deplore.   If sequence of thought is to be preserved, succinctness of expression must now and then be sacrificed.   There can be no reasonable objection to "It was an overhanging cliff with boats below it," yet this seems flat beside the impressionistic elegance of *"C'était une falaise surplombant des bateaux."*   Flaubert's special terminologies have been handled resourcefully, yet there is no way of rendering his colloquial inflections.   In half a dozen instances, where there has been a slip, I have taken the liberty of correcting it. One instance may be worth mentioning.   When Mr. McDowall wrote that the moats of Julian's castle were "full of water," he was conscientiously translating his original.   Flaubert had actually written *"pleins d'herbe,"* and these words appear on a page of the manuscript which is reproduced in the Conard edition.   But all the other editions, from his own publisher's (Charpentier) to recent critical texts (Centenaire, Pléïade), seem to read *"pleins d'eau."* No one, apparently, has questioned the judgment of the typesetters who preferred water to grass, ignoring the peaceful setting, the unlowered portcullis (*herse*), and the bird retrieved a few pages later.   If anyone else except Flaubert had suffered this treatment, it might have been passed over in silence; but that the wrong word should have entrenched itself in the very arcanum of the *mot juste* is an irony which his indignant ghost will forgive us, I hope, for enjoying.

HARRY LEVIN

February 29, 1944

A SIMPLE HEART

A Simple Heart

I

Madame Aubain's servant Félicité was the envy of the ladies of Pont-l'Évêque for half a century.

She received four pounds a year. For that she was cook and general servant, and did the sewing, washing, and ironing; she could bridle a horse, fatten poultry, and churn butter—and she remained faithful to her mistress, unamiable as the latter was.

Mme. Aubain had married a gay bachelor without money who died at the beginning of 1809, leaving her with two small children and a quantity of debts. She then sold all her property except the farms of Toucques and Geffosses, which brought in two hundred pounds a year at most, and left her house in Saint-Melaine for a less expensive one that had belonged to her family and was situated behind the market.

This house had a slate roof and stood between an alley and a lane that went down to the river. There was an unevenness in the levels of the rooms which made you stumble. A narrow hall divided the kitchen from the "parlour" where Mme. Aubain spent her day, sitting in a wicker easy chair by the window. Against the panels, which were painted white, was a row of eight mahogany chairs. On an old piano under the barometer a heap of wooden and cardboard boxes rose like a pyramid. A stuffed armchair stood on either side of the Louis-Quinze chimney-piece, which was in yellow marble with a clock in the middle of it modelled like a temple of Vesta. The whole room was a little musty, as the floor was lower than the garden.

The first floor began with "Madame's" room: very large, with a pale-flowered wall-paper and a portrait of "Monsieur" as a dandy of the period. It led to a smaller room, where there were two children's cots without mattresses. Next came the drawing-room, which was always shut up and full of furniture covered with sheets. Then there was a corridor leading to a study. The shelves of a large bookcase were respectably lined with books and papers, and its three wings surrounded a broad writing-table in darkwood. The two panels at the end of the room were covered with pen-drawings, water-colour landscapes, and engravings by Audran, all relics of better days and vanished splendour. Félicité's room on the top floor got its light from a dormer-window, which looked over the meadows.

She rose at daybreak to be in time for Mass, and worked till evening without stopping. Then, when dinner was over, the plates and dishes in order, and the door shut fast, she thrust the log under the ashes and went to sleep in front of the hearth with her rosary in her hand. Félicité was the stubbornest of all bargainers; and as for cleanness, the polish on her saucepans was the despair of other servants. Thrifty in all things, she ate slowly, gathering off the table in her fingers the crumbs of her loaf—a twelve-pound loaf expressly baked for her, which lasted for three weeks.

At all times of year she wore a print hand-kerchief fastened with a pin behind, a bonnet that covered her hair, grey stockings, a red skirt, and a bibbed apron—such as hospital nurses wear—over her jacket.

Her face was thin and her voice sharp. At twenty-five she looked like forty. From fifty onwards she seemed of no particular age; and with her silence, straight figure, and precise movements she was like a woman made of wood, and going by clockwork.

II

She had had her love-story like another.

Her father, a mason, had been killed by falling off some scaffolding. Then her mother died, her sisters scattered, and a farmer took her in and employed her, while she was still quite little, to herd the cows at pasture. She shivered in rags and would lie flat on the ground to drink water from the ponds; she was beaten for nothing, and finally turned out for the theft of a shilling which she did not steal. She went to another farm, where she became dairy-maid; and as she was liked by her employers her companions were jealous of her.

One evening in August (she was then eighteen) they took her to the assembly at Colleville. She was dazed and stupefied in an instant by the noise of the fiddlers, the lights in the trees, the gay medley of dresses, the lace, the gold crosses, and the throng of people jigging all together. While she kept shyly apart a young man with a well-to-do air, who was leaning on the shaft of a cart and smoking his pipe, came up to ask her to dance. He treated her

to cider, coffee, and cake, and bought her a
silk handkerchief; and then, imagining she had
guessed his meaning, offered to see her home.
At the edge of a field of oats he pushed her
roughly down. She was frightened and began
to cry out; and he went off.

One evening later she was on the Beaumont
road. A big hay-wagon was moving slowly
along; she wanted to get in front of it, and as
she brushed past the wheels she recognized
Theodore. He greeted her quite calmly, saying she must excuse it all because it was "the
fault of the drink." She could not think of
any answer and wanted to run away.

He began at once to talk about the harvest
and the worthies of the commune, for his father had left Colleville for the farm at Les
Écots, so that now he and she were neighbours.
"Ah!" she said. He added that they thought
of settling him in life. Well, he was in no
hurry; he was waiting for a wife to his fancy.
She dropped her head; and then he asked her
if she thought of marrying. She answered
with a smile that it was mean to make fun of
her.

"But I am not, I swear!"—and he passed
his left hand round her waist. She walked in
the support of his embrace; their steps grew

slower. The wind was soft, the stars glittered, the huge wagon-load of hay swayed in front of them, and dust rose from the dragging steps of the four horses. Then, without a word of command, they turned to the right. He clasped her once more in his arms, and she disappeared into the shadow.

The week after Theodore secured some assignations with her.

They met at the end of farmyards, behind a wall, or under a solitary tree. She was not innocent as young ladies are—she had learned knowledge from the animals—but her reason and the instinct of her honour would not let her fall. Her resistance exasperated Theodore's passion; so much so that to satisfy it— or perhaps quite artlessly—he made her an offer of marriage. She was in doubt whether to trust him, but he swore great oaths of fidelity.

Soon he confessed to something troublesome; the year before his parents had bought him a substitute for the army, but any day he might be taken again, and the idea of serving was a terror to him. Félicité took this cowardice of his as a sign of affection, and it redoubled hers. She stole away at night to see him, and when she reached their meeting-place Theodore racked her with his anxieties and urgings.

At last he declared that he would go himself to the prefecture for information, and would tell her the result on the following Sunday, between eleven and midnight.

When the moment came she sped towards her lover. Instead of him she found one of his friends.

He told her that she would not see Theodore any more. To ensure himself against conscription he had married an old woman, Madame Lehoussais, of Toucques, who was very rich.

There was an uncontrollable burst of grief. She threw herself on the ground, screamed, called to the God of mercy, and moaned by herself in the fields till daylight came. Then she came back to the farm and announced that she was going to leave; and at the end of the month she received her wages, tied all her small belongings with a handkerchief, and went to Pont-l'Évêque.

In front of the inn there she made inquiries of a woman in a widow's cap, who, as it happened, was just looking for a cook. The girl did not know much, but her willingness seemed so great and her demands so small that Mme. Aubain ended by saying:

"Very well, then, I will take you."

A quarter of an hour afterwards Félicité was installed in her house.

She lived there at first in a tremble, as it were, at "the style of the house" and the memory of "Monsieur" floating over it all. Paul and Virginie, the first aged seven and the other hardly four, seemed to her beings of a precious substance; she carried them on her back like a horse; it was a sorrow to her that Mme. Aubain would not let her kiss them every minute. And yet she was happy there. Her grief had melted in the pleasantness of things all round.

Every Thursday regular visitors came in for a game of boston, and Félicité got the cards and foot-warmers ready beforehand. They arrived punctually at eight and left before the stroke of eleven.

On Monday mornings the dealer who lodged in the covered passage spread out all his old iron on the ground. Then a hum of voices began to fill the town, mingled with the neighing of horses, bleating of lambs, grunting of pigs, and the sharp rattle of carts along the street. About noon, when the market was at its height, you might see a tall, hook-nosed old countryman with his cap pushed back making his appearance at the door. It was Robelin, the farmer of Geffosses. A little later came Liébard, the farmer from Toucques—short, red, and corpulent—in a grey jacket and gaiters shod with spurs.

Both had poultry or cheese to offer their landlord. Félicité was invariably a match for their cunning, and they went away filled with respect for her.

At vague intervals Mme. Aubain had a visit from the Marquis de Gremanville, one of her uncles, who had ruined himself by debauchery and now lived at Falaise on his last remaining morsel of land. He invariably came at the luncheon hour, with a dreadful poodle whose paws left all the furniture in a mess. In spite of efforts to show his breeding, which he carried to the point of raising his hat every time he mentioned "my late father," habit was to strong for him; he poured himself out glass after glass and fired off improper remarks. Félicité edged him politely out of the house—"You have had enough, Monsieur de Gremanville! Another time!"—and she shut the door on him.

She opened it with pleasure to M. Bourais,

who had been a lawyer. His baldness, his white stock, frilled shirt, and roomy brown coat, his way of rounding the arm as he took snuff—his whole person, in fact, created that disturbance of mind which overtakes us at the sight of extraordinary men.

As he looked after the property of "Madame" he remained shut up with her for hours in "Monsieur's" study, though all the time he was afraid of compromising himself. He respected the magistracy immensely, and had some pretensions to Latin.

To combine instruction and amusement he gave the children a geography book made up of a series of prints. They represented scenes in different parts of the world: cannibals with feathers on their heads, a monkey carrying off a young lady, Bedouins in the desert, the harpooning of a whale, and so on. Paul explained these engravings to Félicité; and that, in fact, was the whole of her literary education. The children's education was undertaken by Guyot, a poor creature employed at the town hall, who was famous for his beautiful hand and sharpened his penknife on his boots.

When the weather was bright the household set off early for a day at Geffosses Farm.

Its courtyard is on a slope, with the farm-house in the middle, and the sea looks like a grey streak in the distance.

Félicité brought slices of cold meat out of her basket, and they breakfasted in a room adjoining the dairy. It was the only surviv-ing fragment of a country house which was now no more. The wall-paper hung in tat-ters, and quivered in the draughts. Mme. Aubain sat with bowed head, overcome by her memories; the children became afraid to speak. "Why don't you play, then?" she would say, and off they went.

Paul climbed into the barn, caught birds, played at ducks and drakes over the pond, or hammered with his stick on the big casks which boomed like drums. Virginie fed the rabbits or dashed off to pick cornflowers, her quick legs showing their embroidered little drawers.

One autumn evening they went home by the fields. The moon was in its first quarter, lighting part of the sky; and mist floated like a scarf over the windings of the Toucques. Cattle, lying out in the middle of the grass, looked quietly at the four people as they passed. In the third meadow some of them got up and made a half-circle in front of the walkers. "There's nothing to be afraid of," said

Félicité, as she stroked the nearest on the back
with a kind of crooning song; he wheeled
round and the others did the same. But when
they crossed the next pasture there was a
formidable bellow. It was a bull, hidden by
the mist. Mme. Aubain was about to run.
"No! no! don't go so fast!" They mended
their pace, however, and heard a loud breathing behind them which came nearer. His
hoofs thudded on the meadow grass like ham-
mers; why, he was galloping now! Félicité
turned round, and tore up clods of earth with
both hands and threw them in his eyes. He
lowered his muzzle, waved his horns, and
quivered with fury, bellowing terribly. Mme.
Aubain, now at the end of the pasture with her
two little ones, was looking wildly for a place
to get over the high bank. Félicité was re-
treating, still with her face to the bull, keeping up a shower of clods which blinded him,
and crying all the time, "Be quick! be quick!"

Mme. Aubain went down into the ditch,
pushed Virginie first and then Paul, fell several times as she tried to climb the bank, and
managed it at last by dint of courage.

The bull had driven Félicité to bay against
a rail-fence; his slaver was streaming into her
face; another second, and he would have gored

her. She had just time to slip between two of the rails, and the big animal stopped short in amazement.

This adventure was talked of at Pont-l'Évêque for many a year. Félicité did not pride herself on it in the least, not having the barest suspicion that she had done anything heroic.

Virginie was the sole object of her thoughts, for the child developed a nervous complaint as a result of her fright, and M. Poupart, the doctor, advised sea-bathing at Trouville. It was not a frequented place then. Mme. Aubain collected information, consulted Bourais, and made preparations as though for a long journey.

Her luggage started a day in advance, in Liébard's cart. The next day he brought round two horses, one of which had a lady's saddle with a velvet back to it, while a cloak was rolled up to make a kind of seat on the crupper of the other. Mme. Aubain rode on that, behind the farmer. Félicité took charge of Virginie, and Paul mounted M. Lechaptois' donkey, lent on condition that great care was taken of it.

The road was so bad that its five miles took two hours. The horses sank in the mud up to

their pasterns, and their haunches jerked
abruptly in the effort to get out; or else they
stumbled in the ruts, and at other moments had
to jump. In some places Liébard's mare
came suddenly to a halt. He waited patiently
until she went on again, talking about the people who had properties along the road, and
adding moral reflections to their history. So
it was that as they were in the middle of
Toucques, and passed under some windows
bowered with nasturtiums, he shrugged his
shoulders and said: "There's a Mme. Lehoussais lives there; instead of taking a young
man she . . ." Félicité did not hear the
rest; the horses were trotting and the donkey
galloping. They all turned down a bypath;
a gate swung open and two boys appeared;
and the party dismounted in front of a manure-
heap at the very threshold of the farmhouse
door.

When Mme. Liébard saw her mistress she
gave lavish signs of joy. She served her a
luncheon with a sirloin of beef, tripe, black-
pudding, a fricassee of chicken, sparkling cider,
a fruit tart, and brandied plums; seasoning it
all with compliments to Madame, who seemed
in better health; Mademoiselle, who was
"splendid" now; and Monsieur Paul, who had

"filled out" wonderfully. Nor did she forget their deceased grandparents, whom the Liébards had known, as they had been in the service of the family for several generations. The farm, like them, had the stamp of antiquity. The beams on the ceiling were worm-eaten, the walls blackened with smoke, and the window-panes grey with dust. There was an oak dresser laden with every sort of useful article—jugs, plates, pewter bowls, wolf-traps, and sheep-shears; and a huge syringe made the children laugh. There was not a tree in the three courtyards without mushrooms growing at the bottom of it or a tuft of mistletoe on its boughs. Several of them had been thrown down by the wind. They had taken root again at the middle; and all were bending under their wealth of apples. The thatched roofs, like brown velvet and of varying thickness, withstood the heaviest squalls. The cart-shed, however, was falling into ruin. Mme. Aubain said she would see about it, and ordered the animals to be saddled again.

It was another half-hour before they reached Trouville. The little caravan dismounted to pass Écores—it was an overhanging cliff with boats below it—and three minutes later they were at the end of the quay

and entered the courtyard of the Golden
Lamb, kept by good Mme. David.

From the first days of their stay Virginie
began to feel less weak, thanks to the change
of air and the effect of the sea-baths. These,
for want of a bathing-dress, she took in her
chemise; and her nurse dressed her afterwards
in a coastguard's cabin which was used by the
bathers.

In the afternoons they took the donkey and
went off beyond the Black Rocks, in the direction of Hennequeville. The path climbed at
first through ground with dells in it like the
green sward of a park, and then reached a
plateau where grass fields and arable lay side
by side. Hollies rose stiffly out of the briary
tangle at the edge of the road; and here and
there a great withered tree made zigzags in
the blue air with its branches.

They nearly always rested in a meadow,
with Deauville on their left, Havre on their
right, and the open sea in front. It glittered
in the sunshine, smooth as a mirror and so
quiet that its murmur was scarcely to be heard;
sparrows chirped in hiding and the immense
sky arched over it all. Mme. Aubain sat
doing her needlework; Virginie plaited rushes

by her side; Félicité pulled up lavender, and
Paul was bored and anxious to start home.

Other days they crossed the Toucques in a
boat and looked for shells. When the tide
went out sea-urchins, starfish, and jelly-fish were
left exposed; and the children ran in pursuit
of the foam-flakes which scudded in the wind.
The sleepy waves broke on the sand and unrolled all along the beach; it stretched away
out of sight, bounded on the land-side by the
dunes which parted it from the Marsh, a wide
meadow shaped like an arena. As they came
home that way, Trouville, on the hill-slope in
the background, grew bigger at every step,
and its miscellaneous throng of houses seemed
to break into a gay disorder.

On days when it was too hot they did not
leave their room. From the dazzling bril-
liance outside light fell in streaks between the
laths of the blinds. There were no sounds in
the village; and on the pavement below not a
soul. This silence round them deepened the
quietness of things. In the distance, where
men were caulking, there was a tap of ham-
mers as they plugged the hulls, and a sluggish
breeze wafted up the smell of tar.

The chief amusement was the return of the

fishing-boats. They began to tack as soon as they had passed the buoys. The sails came down on two of the three masts; and they drew on with the foresail swelling like a balloon, glided through the splash of the waves, and when they had reached the middle of the harbour suddenly dropped anchor. Then the boats drew up against the quay. The sailors threw quivering fish over the side; a row of carts was waiting, and women in cotton bonnets darted out to take the baskets and give their men a kiss.

One of them came up to Félicité one day, and she entered the lodgings a little later in a state of delight. She had found a sister again—and then Nastasie Barette, "wife of Leroux," appeared, holding an infant at her breast and another child with her right hand, while on her left was a little cabin boy with his hands on his hips and a cap over his ear.

After a quarter of an hour Mme. Aubain sent them off; but they were always to be found hanging about the kitchen, or encountered in the course of a walk. The husband never appeared.

Félicité was seized with affection for them. She bought them a blanket, some shirts, and a stove; it was clear that they were making a good thing out of her. Mme. Aubain was annoyed by this weakness of hers, and she did not like the liberties taken by the nephew, who said "thee" and "thou" to Paul. So as Virginie was coughing and the fine weather gone, she returned to Pont-l'Évêque.

There M. Bourais enlightened her on the choice of a boys' school. The one at Caen was reputed to be the best, and Paul was sent to it. He said his good-byes bravely, content enough at going to live in a house where he would have companions.

Mme. Aubain resigned herself to her son's absence as a thing that had to be. Virginie thought about it less and less. Félicité missed the noise he made. But she found an occupation to distract her; from Christmas onward she took the little girl to catechism every day.

III

After making a genuflexion at the door she walked up between the double row of chairs under the lofty nave, opened Mme. Aubain's pew, sat down, and began to look about her. The choir stalls were filled with the boys on the right and the girls on the left, and the curé stood by the lectern. On a painted window in the apse the Holy Ghost looked down upon the Virgin. Another window showed her on her knees before the child Jesus, and a group carved in wood behind the altar-shrine represented St. Michael overthrowing the dragon.

The priest began with a sketch of sacred history. The Garden, the Flood, the Tower of Babel, cities in flames, dying nations, and overturned idols passed like a dream before her eyes; and the dizzying vision left her with reverence for the Most High and fear of his wrath. Then she wept at the story of the Passion. Why had they crucified Him, when He loved the children, fed the multitudes, healed the blind, and had willed, in His meekness, to be born among the poor, on the dung-heap of a stable? The sowings, harvests, wine-presses, all the familiar things the Gospel speaks of, were a part of her life. They had been made holy by God's passing; and she loved the lambs more tenderly for her love of the Lamb, and the doves because of the Holy Ghost.

She found it hard to imagine Him in person, for He was not merely a bird, but a flame as well, and a breath at other times. It may be

His light, she thought, which flits at night about the edge of the marshes, His breathing which drives on the clouds, His voice which gives harmony to the bells; and she would sit rapt in adoration, enjoying the cool walls and the quiet of the church.

Of doctrines she understood nothing—did not even try to understand. The curé discoursed, the children repeated their lesson, and finally she went to sleep, waking up with a start when their wooden shoes clattered on the flagstones as they went away.

It was thus that Félicité, whose religious education had been neglected in her youth, learned the catechism by dint of hearing it; and from that time she copied all Virginie's observances, fasting as she did and confessing with her. On Corpus Christi Day they made a festal altar together.

The first communion loomed distractingly ahead. She fussed over the shoes, the rosary, the book and gloves; and how she trembled as she helped Virginie's mother to dress her!

All through the mass she was racked with anxiety. She could not see one side of the choir because of M. Bourais; but straight in front of her was the flock of maidens, with white crowns above their hanging veils, mak-

ing the impression of a field of snow; and she
knew her dear child at a distance by her dainty
neck and thoughtful air. The bell tinkled.
The heads bowed, and there was silence. As
the organ pealed, singers and congregation
took up the "Agnus Dei"; then the procession
of the boys began, and after them the girls
rose. Step by step, with their hands joined in
prayer, they went towards the lighted altar,
knelt on the first step, received the sacrament
in turn, and came back in the same order to
their places. When Virginie's turn came Félicité leaned forward to see her; and with the
imaginativeness of deep and tender feeling it
seemed to her that she actually was the child;
Virginie's face became hers, she was dressed
in her clothes, it was her heart beating in her
breast. As the moment came to open her
mouth she closed her eyes and nearly fainted.

She appeared early in the sacristy next morning for Monsieur the curé to give her the communion. She took it with devotion, but it
did not give her the same exquisite delight.

Mme. Aubain wanted to make her daughter
into an accomplished person; and as Guyot
could not teach her music or English she decided to place her in the Ursuline Convent at
Honfleur as a boarder. The child made no

objection. Félicité sighed and thought that
Madame lacked feeling. Then she reflected
that her mistress might be right; matters of
this kind were beyond her.

So one day an old spring-van drew up at
the door, and out of it stepped a nun to fetch
the young lady. Félicité hoisted the luggage
on to the top, admonished the driver, and put
six pots of preserves, a dozen pears, and a
bunch of violets under the seat.

At the last moment Virginie broke into a fit
of sobbing; she threw her arms round her
mother, who kissed her on the forehead, saying over and over "Come, be brave! be
brave!" The step was raised, and the carriage drove off.

Then Mme. Aubain's strength gave way;
and in the evening all her friends—the Lormeau family, Mme. Lechaptois, the Rochefeuille ladies, M. de Houppeville, and Bourais—came in to console her.

To be without her daughter was very pain-
ful for her at first. But she heard from Virginie three times a week, wrote to her on the
other days, walked in the garden, and so filled
up the empty hours.

From sheer habit Félicité went into Virginie's room in the mornings and gazed at

the walls. It was boredom to her not to have
to comb the child's hair now, lace up her boots,
tuck her into bed—and not to see her charming
face perpetually and hold her hand when they
went out together. In this idle condition she
tried making lace. But her fingers were too
heavy and broke the threads; she could not
attend to anything, she had lost her sleep, and
was, in her own words, "destroyed."

To "divert herself" she asked leave to have
visits from her nephew Victor.

He arrived on Sundays after mass, rosy-
cheeked, bare-chested, with the scent of the
country he had walked through still about him.
She laid her table promptly and they had lunch,
sitting opposite each other. She ate as little
as possible herself to save expense, but stuffed
him with food so generously that at last he
went to sleep. At the first stroke of vespers
she woke him up, brushed his trousers, fastened his tie, and went to church, leaning on his
arm with maternal pride.

Victor was always instructed by his parents
to get something out of her—a packet of moist
sugar, it might be, a cake of soap, spirits, or
even money at times. He brought his things
for her to mend and she took over the task,

only too glad to have a reason for making him come back.

In August his father took him off on a coasting voyage. It was holiday time, and she was consoled by the arrival of the children. Paul, however, was getting selfish, and Virginie was too old to be called "thou" any longer; this put a constraint and barrier between them.

Victor went to Morlaix, Dunkirk, and Brighton in succession and made Félicité a present on his return from each voyage. It was a box made of shells the first time, a coffee cup the next, and on the third occasion a large gingerbread man. Victor was growing handsome. He was well made, had a hint of a moustache, good honest eyes, and a small leather hat pushed backwards like a pilot's. He entertained her by telling stories embroidered with nautical terms.

On a Monday, July 14, 1819 (she never forgot the date), he told her that he had signed on for the big voyage and next night but one he would take the Honfleur boat and join his schooner, which was to weigh anchor from Havre before long. Perhaps he would be gone two years.

The prospect of this long absence threw

Félicité into deep distress; one more good-bye
she must have, and on the Wednesday evening, when Madame's dinner was finished, she
put on her clogs and made short work of the
twelve miles between Pont-l'Évêque and
Honfleur.

When she arrived in front of the Calvary
she took the turn to the right instead of the
left, got lost in the timber-yards, and retraced
her steps; some people to whom she spoke advised her to be quick. She went all round the
harbour basin, full of ships, and knocked
against hawsers; then the ground fell away,
lights flashed across each other, and she
thought her wits had left her, for she saw
horses up in the sky.

Others were neighing by the quay-side,
frightened at the sea. They were lifted by a
tackle and deposited in a boat, where passengers jostled each other among cider casks,
cheese baskets, and sacks of grain; fowls could
be heard clucking, the captain swore; and a
cabin-boy stood leaning over the bows, indif-
ferent to it all. Félicité, who had not recognized him, called "Victor!" and he raised his
head; all at once, as she was darting forwards,
the gangway was drawn back.

The Honfleur packet, women singing as they

hauled it, passed out of harbour. Its frame-
work creaked and the heavy waves whipped its
bows. The canvas had swung round, no one
could be seen on board now; and on the moon-
silvered sea the boat made a black speck which
paled gradually, dipped, and vanished.

As Félicité passed by the Calvary she had a
wish to commend to God what she cherished
most, and she stood there praying a long time
with her face bathed in tears and her eyes towards the clouds. The town was asleep,
coastguards were walking to and fro; and
water poured without cessation through the
holes in the sluice, with the noise of a torrent.
The clocks struck two.

The convent parlour would not be open
before day. If Félicité were late Madame
would most certainly be annoyed; and in spite
of her desire to kiss the other child she turned
home. The maids at the inn were waking up
as she came in to Pont-l'Évêque.

So the poor slip of a boy was going to toss
for months and months at sea! She had not
been frightened by his previous voyages.
From England or Brittany you came back safe
enough; but America, the colonies, the is-
lands—these were lost in a dim region at the
other end of the world.

Félicité's thoughts from that moment ran entirely on her nephew. On sunny days she was harassed by the idea of thirst; when there was a storm she was afraid of the lightning on his account. As she listened to the wind growling in the chimney or carrying off the slates she pictured him lashed by that same tempest, at the top of a shattered mast, with his body thrown backwards under a sheet of foam; or else (with a reminiscence of the illustrated geography) he was being eaten by savages, captured in a wood by monkeys, or dying on a desert shore. And never did she mention her anxieties.

Mme. Aubain had anxieties of her own, about her daughter. The good sisters found her an affectionate but delicate child. The slightest emotion unnerved her. She had to give up the piano.

Her mother stipulated for regular letters from the convent. She lost patience one morning when the postman did not come, and walked to and fro in the parlour from her armchair to the window. It was really amazing; not a word for four days!

To console Mme. Aubain by her own example Félicité remarked:

"As for me, Madame, it's six months since I heard . . ."

"From whom, pray?"

"Why . . . from my nephew," the servant answered gently.

"Oh! your nephew!" And Mme. Aubain resumed her walk with a shrug of the shoulders, as much as to say: "I was not thinking of him! And what is more, it's absurd! A scamp of a cabin-boy—what does he matter? . . . whereas my daughter . . . why, just think!"

Félicité, though she had been brought up on harshness, felt indignant with Madame— and then forgot. It seemed the simplest thing in the world to her to lose one's head over the little girl. For her the two children were equally important; a bond in her heart made them one, and their destinies must be the same.

She heard from the chemist that Victor's ship had arrived at Havana. He had read this piece of news in a gazette.

Cigars—they made her imagine Havana as a place where no one does anything but smoke, and there was Victor moving among the negroes in a cloud of tobacco. Could you, she wondered, "in case you needed," return by land? What was the distance from Pont-l'-Évêque? She questioned M. Bourais to find out.

He reached for his atlas and began explaining the longitudes; Félicité's consternation provoked a fine pedantic smile. Finally he marked with his pencil a black, imperceptible point in the indentations of an oval spot, and said as he did so, "Here it is." She bent over the map; the maze of coloured lines wearied her eyes without conveying anything; and on an invitation from Bourais to tell him her difficulty she begged him to show her the house where Victor was living. Bourais threw up his arms, sneezed, and laughed immensely: a simplicity like hers was a positive joy. And Félicité did not understand the reason; how could she when she expected, very likely, to see the actual image of her nephew—so stunted was her mind!

A fortnight afterwards Liébard came into the kitchen at market-time as usual and handed her a letter from her brother-in-law. As neither of them could read she took it to her mistress.

Mme. Aubain, who was counting the stitches in her knitting, put the work down by her side, broke the seal of the letter, started, and said in a low voice, with a look of meaning:

"It is bad news . . . that they have to tell you. Your nephew . . ."

He was dead. The letter said no more.

Félicité fell on to a chair, leaning her head against the wainscot; and she closed her eyelids, which suddenly flushed pink. Then with bent forehead, hands hanging, and fixed eyes, she said at intervals:

"Poor little lad! poor little lad!"

Liébard watched her and heaved sighs. Mme. Aubain trembled a little.

She suggested that Félicité should go to see her sister at Trouville. Félicité answered by a gesture that she had no need.

There was a silence. The worthy Liébard thought it was time for them to withdraw.

Then Félicité said:

"They don't care, not they!"

Her head dropped again; and she took up mechanically, from time to time, the long needles on her work-table.

Women passed in the yard with a barrow of dripping linen.

As she saw them through the window-panes she remembered her washing; she had put it to soak the day before, to-day she must wring it out; and she left the room.

Her plank and tub were at the edge of the Toucques. She threw a pile of linen on the bank, rolled up her sleeves, and taking her wooden beater dealt lusty blows whose sound carried to the neighbouring gardens. The meadows were empty, the river stirred in the wind; and down below long grasses wavered, like the hair of corpses floating in the water. She kept her grief down and was very brave until the evening; but once in her room she surrendered to it utterly, lying stretched on the mattress with her face in the pillow and her hands clenched against her temples.

Much later she heard, from the captain himself, the circumstances of Victor's end. They had bled him too much at the hospital for yellow fever. Four doctors held him at once. He had died instantly, and the chief had said:

"Bah! there goes another!"

His parents had always been brutal to him. She preferred not to see them again; and they made no advances, either because they forgot her or from the callousness of the wretchedly poor.

Virginie began to grow weaker.

Tightness in her chest, coughing, continual fever, and veinings on her cheek-bones betrayed some deep-seated complaint. M. Poupart had advised a stay in Provence. Mme. Aubain determined on it, and would have brought her daughter home at once but for the climate of Pont-l'Évêque.

She made an arrangement with a job-master, and he drove her to the convent every Tuesday. There is a terrace in the garden, with a view over the Seine. Virginie took walks there over the fallen vine-leaves, on her mother's arm. A shaft of sunlight through the clouds made her blink sometimes, as she gazed at the sails in the distance and the whole horizon from the castle of Tancarville to the lighthouses at Havre. Afterwards they rested in the arbour. Her mother had secured a little cask of excellent Malaga; and Virginie, laughing at the idea of getting tipsy, drank a thimble-full of it, no more.

Her strength came back visibly. The autumn glided gently away. Félicité reassured Mme. Aubain. But one evening, when she had been out on a commission in the neighbourhood, she found M. Poupart's gig at the door. He was in the hall, and Mme. Aubain was tying her bonnet.

"Give me my foot-warmer, purse, gloves! Quicker, come!"

Virginie had inflammation of the lungs; perhaps it was hopeless.

"Not yet!" said the doctor, and they both got into the carriage under whirling flakes of snow. Night was coming on and it was very cold.

Félicité rushed into the church to light a taper. Then she ran after the gig, came up with it in an hour, and jumped lightly in behind. As she hung on by the fringes a thought came into her mind: "The courtyard has not been shut up; supposing burglars got in!" And she jumped down.

At dawn next day she presented herself at the doctor's. He had come in and started for the country again. Then she waited in the inn, thinking that a letter would come by some hand or other. Finally, when it was twilight, she took the Lisieux coach.

The convent was at the end of a steep lane. When she was about half-way up it she heard strange sounds—a death-bell tolling. "It is for someone else," thought Félicité, and she pulled the knocker violently.

After some minutes there was a sound of

trailing slippers, the door opened ajar, and a nun appeared.

The good sister, with an air of compunction, said that "she had just passed away." On the instant the bell of St. Leonard's tolled twice as fast.

Félicité went up to the second floor.

From the doorway she saw Virginie stretched on her back, with her hands joined, her mouth open, and head thrown back under a black crucifix that leaned towards her, between curtains that hung stiffly, less pale than was her face. Mme. Aubain, at the foot of the bed which she clasped with her arms, was choking with sobs of agony. The mother superior stood on the right. Three candlesticks on the chest of drawers made spots of red, and the mist came whitely through the windows. Nuns came and took Mme. Aubain away.

For two nights Félicité never left the dead child. She repeated the same prayers, sprinkled holy water over the sheets, came and sat down again, and watched her. At the end of the first vigil she noticed that the face had grown yellow, the lips turned blue, the nose was sharper, and the eyes sunk in. She kissed them several times, and would not have been immensely surprised if Virginie had opened them again; to minds like hers the supernatural is quite simple. She made the girl's toilette, wrapped her in her shroud, lifted her down into her bier, put a garland on her head, and spread out her hair. It was fair, and extraordinarily long for her age. Félicité cut off a big lock and slipped half of it into her bosom, determined that she should never part with it.

The body was brought back to Pont-l'Évêque, as Mme. Aubain intended; she followed the hearse in a closed carriage.

It took another three-quarters of an hour after the mass to reach the cemetery. Paul walked in front, sobbing. M. Bourais was behind, and then came the chief residents, the women shrouded in black mantles, and Félicité. She thought of her nephew; and because she had not been able to pay these honours to him her grief was doubled, as though the one were being buried with the other.

Mme. Aubain's despair was boundless. It was against God that she first rebelled, thinking it unjust of Him to have taken her daughter from her—she had never done evil and her conscience was so clear! Ah, no!—she ought to have taken Virginie off to the south. Other doctors would have saved her. She accused herself now, wanted to join her child, and broke into cries of distress in the middle of her dreams. One dream haunted her above all. Her husband, dressed as a sailor, was returning from a long voyage, and shedding tears he told her that he had been ordered to take Virginie away. Then they consulted how to hide her somewhere.

She came in once from the garden quite upset. A moment ago—and she pointed out the place—the father and daughter had appeared to her, standing side by side, and they did nothing, but they looked at her.

For several months after this she stayed inertly in her room. Félicité lectured her gently; she must live for her son's sake, and for the other, in remembrance of "her."

"Her?" answered Mme. Aubain, as though she were just waking up. "Ah, yes! . . . yes! . . . You do not forget her!" This was an allusion to the cemetery, where she was strictly forbidden to go.

Félicité went there every day.

Precisely at four she skirted the houses, climbed the hill, opened the gate, and came to Virginie's grave. It was a little column of pink marble with a stone underneath and a garden plot enclosed by chains. The beds were hidden under a coverlet of flowers. She watered their leaves, freshened the gravel, and knelt down to break up the earth better. When Mme. Aubain was able to come there she felt a relief and a sort of consolation.

Then years slipped away, one like another, and their only episodes were the great festivals as they recurred—Easter, the Assumption, All Saints' Day. Household occurrences marked dates that were referred to afterwards. In 1825, for instance, two glaziers whitewashed the hall; in 1827 a piece of the roof fell into the courtyard and nearly killed a man. In the summer of 1828 it was Madame's turn to offer the consecrated bread; Bourais, about this time, mysteriously absented himself; and one by one the old acquaintances passed away: Guyot, Liébard, Mme. Lechaptois, Robelin, and Uncle Gremanville, who had been paralysed for a long time.

One night the driver of the mail-coach announced the Revolution of July in Pont-l'Évêque. A new sub-prefect was appointed a few days later—Baron de Larsonnière, who had been consul in America, and brought with him, besides his wife, a sister-in-law and three young ladies, already growing up. They were to be seen about on their lawn, in loose blouses,

and they had a negro and a parrot. They paid
a call on Mme. Aubain which she did not fail
to return. The moment they were seen in the
distance Félicité ran to let her mistress know.
But only one thing could really move her feelings—the letters from her son.

He was swallowed up in a tavern life and
could follow no career. She paid his debts,
he made new ones; and the sighs that Mme.
Aubain uttered as she sat knitting by the window reached Félicité at her spinning-wheel in
the kitchen.

They took walks together along the espal-
iered wall, always talking of Virginie and won-
dering if such and such a thing would have
pleased her and what, on some occasion, she
would have been likely to say.

All her small belongings filled a cupboard
in the two-bedded room. Mme. Aubain inspected them as seldom as she could. One
summer day she made up her mind to it—and
some moths flew out of the wardrobe.

Virginie's dresses were in a row underneath
a shelf, on which there were three dolls, some
hoops, a set of toy pots and pans, and the basin that she used. They took out her petticoats
as well, and the stockings and handkerchiefs,
and laid them out on the two beds before fold-

ing them up again. The sunshine lit up these poor things, bringing out their stains and the creases made by the body's movements. The air was warm and blue, a blackbird warbled, life seemed bathed in a deep sweetness. They found a little plush hat with thick, chestnut-coloured pile; but it was eaten all over by moth. Félicité begged it for her own. Their eyes met fixedly and filled with tears; at last the mistress opened her arms, the servant threw herself into them, and they embraced each other, satisfying their grief in a kiss that made them equal.

It was the first time in their lives, Mme. Aubain's nature not being expansive. Félicité was as grateful as though she had received a favour, and cherished her mistress from that moment with the devotion of an animal and a religious worship.

The kindness of her heart unfolded.

When she heard the drums of a marching regiment in the street she posted herself at the door with a pitcher of cider and asked the soldiers to drink. She nursed cholera patients and protected the Polish refugees; one of these even declared that he wished to marry her. They quarrelled, however; for when she came back from the Angelus one morning she found that he had got into her kitchen and made himself a vinegar salad which he was quietly eating.

After the Poles came father Colmiche, an old man who was supposed to have committed atrocities in '93. He lived by the side of the river in the ruins of a pigsty. The little boys watched him through the cracks in the wall, and threw pebbles at him which fell on the pallet where he lay constantly shaken by a catarrh; his hair was very long, his eyes inflamed, and there was a tumour on his arm bigger than his head. She got him some linen and tried to clean up his miserable hole; her dream was to establish him in the bakehouse, without letting him annoy Madame. When the tumour burst she dressed it every day; sometimes she brought him cake, and would put him in the sunshine on a truss of straw. The poor old man, slobbering and trembling, thanked her in his worn-out voice, was terrified that he might lose her, and stretched out his hands when he saw her go away. He died; and she had a mass said for the repose of his soul.

That very day a great happiness befell her; just at dinner-time appeared Mme. de Larsonnière's negro, carrying the parrot in its cage, with perch, chain, and padlock. A note from the baroness informed Mme. Aubain that her husband had been raised to a prefecture and they were starting that evening; she begged her to accept the bird as a memento and mark of her regard.

For a long time he had absorbed Félicité's imagination, because he came from America; and that name reminded her of Victor, so much so that she made inquiries of the negro.   She had once gone so far as to say "How Madame would enjoy having him!"

The negro repeated the remark to his mistress; and as she could not take the bird away with her she chose this way of getting rid of him.

IV

His name was Loulou.   His body was green and the tips of his wings rose-pink; his forehead was blue and his throat golden.

But he had the tiresome habits of biting his perch, tearing out his feathers, sprinkling his dirt about, and spattering the water of his tub. He annoyed Mme. Aubain, and she gave him to Félicité for good.

She endeavoured to train him; soon he could repeat "Nice boy!   Your servant, sir!   Good morning, Marie!"   He was placed by the side of the door, and astonished several people by not answering to the name Jacquot, for all parrots are called Jacquot. People compared him to a turkey and a log of wood, and stabbed Félicité to the heart each time. Strange obstinacy on Loulou's part!—directly you looked at him he refused to speak.

None the less he was eager for society; for on Sundays, while the Rochefeuille ladies, M. de Houppeville, and new familiars—Onfroy the apothecary, Monsieur Varin, and Captain Mathieu—were playing their game of cards, he beat the windows with his wings and threw himself about so frantically that they could not hear each other speak.

Bourais' face, undoubtedly, struck him as extremely droll. Directly he saw it he began to laugh—and laugh with all his might. His peals rang through the courtyard and were repeated by the echo; the neighbours came to their windows and laughed too; while M. Bourais, gliding along under the wall to escape the parrot's eye, and hiding his profile with his hat, got to the river and then entered by the garden gate. There was a lack of tenderness in the looks which he darted at the bird.

Loulou had been slapped by the butcher-boy for making so free as to plunge his head into his basket; and since then he was always trying to nip him through his shirt. Fabu threatened to wring his neck, although he was not cruel, for all his tattooed arms and large whiskers. Far from it; he really rather liked the parrot, and in a jovial humour even wanted to teach him to swear. Félicité, who was alarmed by such proceedings, put the bird in the kitchen. His little chain was taken off and he roamed about the house.

His way of going downstairs was to lean on each step with the curve of his beak, raise the right foot, and then the left; and Félicité was afraid that these gymnastics brought on fits of giddiness. He fell ill and could not talk or eat any longer. There was a growth under his tongue, such as fowls have sometimes. She cured him by tearing the pellicle off with her finger-nails. Mr. Paul was thoughtless enough one day to blow some cigar smoke into his nostrils, and another time when Mme. Lormeau was teasing him with the end of her umbrella he snapped at the ferrule. Finally he got lost.

Félicité had put him on the grass to refresh him, and gone away for a minute, and when she came back—no sign of the parrot! She began by looking for him in the shrubs, by the

waterside, and over the roofs, without listen-
ing to her mistress's cries of "Take care, do!
You are out of your wits!" Then she investi-
gated all the gardens in Pont-l'Évêque, and
stopped the passers-by. "You don't ever happen to have seen my parrot, by any chance,
do you?" And she gave a description of the
parrot to those who did not know him. Suddenly, behind the mills at the foot of the hill
she thought she could make out something
green that fluttered. But on the top of the
hill there was nothing. A hawker assured her
that he had come across the parrot just before,
at Saint-Melaine, in Mère Simon's shop. She
rushed there; they had no idea of what she
meant. At last she came home exhausted,
with her slippers in shreds and despair in her
soul; and as she was sitting in the middle of
the garden-seat at Madame's side, telling the
whole story of her efforts, a light weight
dropped on to her shoulder—it was Loulou!
What on earth had he been doing? Taking a
walk in the neighbourhood, perhaps!

She had some trouble in recovering from
this, or rather never did recover. As the result of a chill she had an attack of quinsy, and
soon afterwards an earache. Three years
later she was deaf; and she spoke very loud,

even in church. Though Félicité's sins might have been published in every corner of the diocese without dishonour to her or scandal to anybody, his Reverence the priest thought it right now to hear her confession in the sacristy only.

Imaginary noises in the head completed her upset. Her mistress often said to her, "Heavens! how stupid you are!" "Yes, Madame," she replied, and looked about for something.

Her little circle of ideas grew still narrower; the peal of church-bells and the lowing of cattle ceased to exist for her. All living beings moved as silently as ghosts. One sound only reached her ears now—the parrot's voice.

Loulou, as though to amuse her, reproduced the click-clack of the turn-spit, the shrill call of a man selling fish, and the noise of the saw in the joiner's house opposite; when the bell rang he imitated Mme. Aubain's "Félicité! the door! the door!"

They carried on conversations, he endlessly reciting the three phrases in his repertory, to which she replied with words that were just as disconnected but uttered what was in her heart. Loulou was almost a son and a lover to her in her isolated state. He climbed up her fingers, nibbled at her lips, and clung to her kerchief;

and when she bent her forehead and shook her head gently to and fro, as nurses do, the great wings of her bonnet and the bird's wings quivered together.

When the clouds massed and the thunder rumbled Loulou broke into cries, perhaps remembering the downpours in his native forests. The streaming rain made him absolutely mad; he fluttered wildly about, dashed up to the ceiling, upset everything, and went out through the window to dabble in the garden; but he was back quickly to perch on one of the fire-dogs and hopped about to dry himself, exhibiting his tail and his beak in turn.

One morning in the terrible winter of 1837 she had put him in front of the fireplace because of the cold.   She found him dead, in the middle of his cage: head downwards, with his claws in the wires.   He had died from congestion, no doubt.   But Félicité thought he had been poisoned with parsley, and though there was no proof of any kind her suspicions inclined to Fabu.

She wept so piteously that her mistress said to her, "Well, then, have him stuffed!"

She asked advice from the chemist, who had always been kind to the parrot.   He wrote to Havre, and a person called Fellacher under-

took the business. But as parcels sometimes
got lost in the coach she decided to take the
parrot as far as Honfleur herself.

Along the sides of the road were leafless
apple-trees, one after the other. Ice covered
the ditches. Dogs barked about the farms;
and Félicité, with her hands under her cloak,
her little black sabots and her basket, walked
briskly in the middle of the road.

She crossed the forest, passed High Oak,
and reached St. Gatien.

A cloud of dust rose behind her, and in it
a mail-coach, carried away by the steep hill,
rushed down at full gallop like a hurricane.
Seeing this woman who would not get out of
the way, the driver stood up in front and the
postilion shouted too. He could not hold in
his four horses, which increased their pace, and
the two leaders were grazing her when he
threw them to one side with a jerk of the reins.
But he was wild with rage, and lifting his arm
as he passed at full speed, gave her such a lash
from waist to neck with his big whip that she
fell on her back.

Her first act, when she recovered consciousness, was to open her basket. Loulou was
happily none the worse. She felt a burn in her
right cheek, and when she put her hands

against it they were red; the blood was flowing.

She sat down on a heap of stones and bound up her face with her handkerchief. Then she ate a crust of bread which she had put in the basket as a precaution, and found a consolation for her wound in gazing at the bird.

When she reached the crest of Ecquemauville she saw the Honfleur lights sparkling in the night sky like a company of stars; beyond, the sea stretched dimly. Then a faintness overtook her and she stopped; her wretched childhood, the disillusion of her first love, her nephew's going away, and Virginie's death all came back to her at once like the waves of an oncoming tide, rose to her throat, and choked her.

Afterwards, at the boat, she made a point of speaking to the captain, begging him to take care of the parcel, though she did not tell him what was in it.

Fellacher kept the parrot a long time. He was always promising it for the following week. After six months he announced that a packing-case had started, and then nothing more was heard of it. It really seemed as though Loulou was never coming back. "Ah, they have stolen him!" she thought.

He arrived at last, and looked superb.

There he was, erect upon a branch which
screwed into a mahogany socket, with a foot
in the air and his head on one side, biting a
nut which the bird-stuffer—with a taste for im-
pressiveness—had gilded.

Félicité shut him up in her room. It was a
place to which few people were admitted, and
held so many religious objects and miscellaneous things that it looked like a chapel and
bazaar in one.

A big cupboard impeded you as you opened
the door. Opposite the window commanding
the garden a little round one looked into the
court; there was a table by the folding-bed
with a water-jug, two combs, and a cube of
blue soap in a chipped plate. On the walls
hung rosaries, medals, several benign Virgins,
and a holy water vessel made out of cocoa-nut;
on the chest of drawers, which was covered
with a cloth like an altar, was the shell box
that Victor had given her, and after that a
watering-can, a toy-balloon, exercise-books, the
illustrated geography, and a pair of young
lady's boots; and, fastened by its ribbons to
the nail of the looking-glass, hung the little
plush hat! Félicité carried observances of
this kind so far as to keep one of Monsieur's
frock-coats. All the old rubbish which Mme.

Aubain did not want any longer she laid hands on for her room. That was why there were artificial flowers along the edge of the chest of drawers and a portrait of the Comte d'Artois in the little window recess.

With the aid of a bracket Loulou was established over the chimney, which jutted into the room. Every morning when she woke up she saw him there in the dawning light, and recalled old days and the smallest details of insignificant acts in a deep quietness which knew no pain.

Holding, as she did, no communication with anyone, Félicité lived as insensibly as if she were walking in her sleep. The Corpus Christi processions roused her to life again. Then she went round begging mats and candlesticks from the neighbours to decorate the altar they put up in the street.

In church she was always gazing at the Holy Ghost in the window, and observed that there was something of the parrot in him. The likeness was still clearer, she thought, on a crude colour-print representing the baptism of Our Lord. With his purple wings and emerald body he was the very image of Loulou.

She bought him, and hung him up instead of the Comte d'Artois, so that she could see them both together in one glance. They were linked in her thoughts; and the parrot was consecrated by his association with the Holy Ghost, which became more vivid to her eye and more intelligible. The Father could not have chosen to express Himself through a dove, for such creatures cannot speak; it must have been one of Loulou's ancestors, surely. And though Félicité looked at the picture while she said her prayers she swerved a little from time to time towards the parrot.

She wanted to join the Ladies of the Virgin, but Mme. Aubain dissuaded her.

And then a great event loomed up before them—Paul's marriage.

He had been a solicitor's clerk to begin with, and then tried business, the Customs, the Inland Revenue, and made efforts, even, to get into the Rivers and Forests. By an inspiration from heaven he had suddenly, at thirty-six, discovered his real line—the Registrar's Office. And there he showed such marked capacity that an inspector had offered him his daughter's hand and promised him his influence.

So Paul, grown serious, brought the lady to see his mother.

She sniffed at the ways of Pont-l'Évêque, gave herself great airs, and wounded Félicité's feelings. Mme. Aubain was relieved at her departure.

The week after came news of M. Bourais' death in an inn in Lower Brittany. The rumour of suicide was confirmed, and doubts arose as to his honesty. Mme. Aubain studied his accounts, and soon found out the whole tale of his misdoings—embezzled arrears, secret sales of wood, forged receipts, etc. Besides that he had an illegitimate child, and "relations with a person at Dozulé."

These shameful facts distressed her greatly. In March 1853 she was seized with a pain in the chest; her tongue seemed to be covered with film, and leeches did not ease the difficult breathing. On the ninth evening of her illness she died, just at seventy-two.

She passed as being younger, owing to the bands of brown hair which framed her pale, pock-marked face. There were few friends to regret her, for she had a stiffness of manner which kept people at a distance.

But Félicité mourned for her as one seldom mourns for a master. It upset her ideas and seemed contrary to the order of things, impossible and monstrous, that Madame should die before her.

Ten days afterwards, which was the time it

took to hurry there from Besançon, the heirs
arrived. The daughter-in-law ransacked the
drawers, chose some furniture, and sold the
rest; and then they went back to their
registering.

Madame's armchair, her small round table,
her foot-warmer, and the eight chairs were
gone! Yellow patches in the middle of the
panels showed where the engravings had hung.
They had carried off the two little beds and the
mattresses, and all Virginie's belongings had
disappeared from the cupboard. Félicité went
from floor to floor dazed with sorrow.

The next day there was a notice on the door,
and the apothecary shouted in her ear that
the house was for sale.

She tottered, and was obliged to sit down.
What distressed her most of all was to give up
her room, so suitable as it was for poor Loulou. She enveloped him with a look of an-
guish when she was imploring the Holy Ghost,
and formed the idolatrous habit of kneeling
in front of the parrot to say her prayers.
Sometimes the sun shone in at the attic window and caught his glass eye, and a great
luminous ray shot out of it and put her in an
ecstasy.

She had a pension of fifteen pounds a year which her mistress had left her. The garden gave her a supply of vegetables. As for clothes, she had enough to last her to the end of her days, and she economized in candles by going to bed at dusk.

She hardly ever went out, as she did not like passing the dealer's shop, where some of the old furniture was exposed for sale. Since her fit of giddiness she dragged one leg; and as her strength was failing Mère Simon, whose grocery business had collapsed, came every morning to split the wood and pump water for her.

Her eyes grew feeble. The shutters ceased to be thrown open. Years and years passed, and the house was neither let nor sold.

Félicité never asked for repairs because she was afraid of being sent away. The boards on the roof rotted; her bolster was wet for a whole winter. After Easter she spat blood.

Then Mère Simon called in a doctor. Félicité wanted to know what was the matter with her. But she was too deaf to hear, and the only word which reached her was "pneumonia." It was a word she knew, and she answered softly "Ah! like Madame," thinking it natural that she should follow her mistress.

The time for the festal shrines was coming near. The first one was always at the bottom of the hill, the second in front of the post-office, and the third towards the middle of the street. There was some rivalry in the matter of this one, and the women of the parish ended by choosing Mme. Aubain's court-yard.

The hard breathing and fever increased. Félicité was vexed at doing nothing for the altar. If only she could at least have put something there! Then she thought of the parrot. The neighbours objected that it would not be decent. But the priest gave her permission, which so intensely delighted her that she begged him to accept Loulou, her sole possession, when she died.

From Tuesday to Saturday, the eve of the festival, she coughed more often. By the evening her face had shrivelled, her lips stuck to her gums, and she had vomitings; and at twilight next morning, feeling herself very low, she sent for a priest.

Three kindly women were round her during the extreme unction. Then she announced that she must speak to Fabu. He arrived in his

Sunday clothes, by no means at his ease in the funereal atmosphere.

"Forgive me," she said, with an effort to stretch out her arm; "I thought it was you who had killed him."

What did she mean by such stories? She suspected him of murder—a man like him! He waxed indignant, and was on the point of making a row.

"There," said the women, "she is no longer in her senses, you can see it well enough!"

Félicité spoke to shadows of her own from time to time. The women went away, and Mère Simon had breakfast. A little later she took Loulou and brought him close to Félicité with the words:

"Come, now, say good-bye to him!"

Loulou was not a corpse, but the worms devoured him; one of his wings was broken, and the tow was coming out of his stomach. But she was blind now; she kissed him on the forehead and kept him close against her cheek. Mère Simon took him back from her to put him on the altar.

V

Summer scents came up from the meadows; flies buzzed; the sun made the river glitter and heated the slates. Mère Simon came back into the room and fell softly asleep.

She woke at the noise of bells; the people were coming out from vespers. Félicité's delirium subsided. She thought of the procession and saw it as if she had been there.

All the school children, the church-singers, and the firemen walked on the pavement, while in the middle of the road the verger armed with his hallebard and the beadle with a large cross advanced in front. Then came the schoolmaster, with an eye on the boys, and the sister, anxious about her little girls; three of the daintiest, with angelic curls, scattered rose-petals in the air; the deacon controlled the band with outstretched arms; and two censer-bearers turned back at every step towards the Holy Sacrament, which was borne by Monsieur the curé, wearing his beautiful chasuble, under a canopy of dark-red velvet held up by four churchwardens. A crowd of people pressed behind, between the white cloths covering the house walls, and they reached the bottom of the hill.

A cold sweat moistened Félicité's temples. Mère Simon sponged her with a piece of linen, saying to herself that one day she would have to go that way.

The hum of the crowd increased, was very loud for an instant, and then went further away.

A fusillade shook the window-panes. It was the postilions saluting the monstrance. Félicité rolled her eyes and said as audibly as she could: "Does he look well?" The parrot was weighing on her mind.

Her agony began. A death-rattle that grew more and more convulsed made her sides heave. Bubbles of froth came at the corners of her mouth and her whole body trembled.

Soon the booming of the ophicleides, the high voices of the children, and the deep voices of the men were distinguishable. At intervals all was silent, and the tread of feet, deadened by the flowers they walked on, sounded like a flock pattering on grass.

The clergy appeared in the courtyard. Mère Simon clambered on to a chair to reach the attic window, and so looked down straight upon the shrine. Green garlands hung over the altar, which was decked with a flounce of English lace. In the middle was a small frame with relics in it; there were two orange-trees at the corners, and all along stood silver candlesticks and china vases, with sunflowers, lilies, peonies, foxgloves, and tufts of horten-

sia. This heap of blazing colour slanted
from the level of the altar to the carpet which
went on over the pavement; and some rare objects caught the eye. There was a silver-gilt
sugar-basin with a crown of violets; pendants
of Alençon stone glittered on the moss, and
two Chinese screens displayed their landscapes.
Loulou was hidden under roses, and showed
nothing but his blue forehead, like a plaque of
lapis lazuli.

The churchwardens, singers, and children
took their places round the three sides of the
court. The priest went slowly up the steps,
and placed his great, radiant golden sun upon
the lace. Everyone knelt down. There was
a deep silence; and the censers glided to and
fro on the full swing of their chains.

An azure vapour rose up into Félicité's
room. Her nostrils met it; she inhaled it
sensuously, mystically; and then closed her
eyes. Her lips smiled. The beats of her
heart lessened one by one, vaguer each time
and softer, as a fountain sinks, an echo disap-
pears; and when she sighed her last breath
she thought she saw an opening in the heavens,
and a gigantic parrot hovering above her head.

THE LEGEND OF ST. JULIAN
THE HOSPITALLER

The Legend of St. Julian the Hospitaller

I

JULIAN's father and mother lived in a castle with a forest round it, on the slope of a hill.

The four towers at its corners had pointed roofs covered with scales of lead, and the walls were planted upon shafts of rock which fell steeply to the bottom of the moat. The pavement of the courtyard was as clean as the flagstones of a church. Long gutter-spouts in the form of leaning dragons spat the rain-water down into the cistern; and on the window-ledges of each storey, in pots of painted earthenware, a heliotrope or basil flowered.

A second enclosure made with stakes held a fruit-orchard to begin with, and then a flower garden patterned into figures; then a trellis with arbours where you took the air, and an alley for the pages to play mall. On the other side were the kennels, the stables, the bake-house, the presses, and the barns. A green and turfy pasture spread all round this, enclosed in turn by a stout thorn-hedge.

They had lived at peace so long that the portcullis was never lowered now. The moats were full of grass; swallows nested in the cracks of the battlements; and when the sun blazed too strongly the archer who paced all day long the rampart took refuge in his turret and slept like a monk.

Inside there was a sheen of ironwork everywhere; the rooms were hung with tapestries against the cold; the cupboards overflowed with linen; casks of wine were piled up in the cellars, and the oaken coffers creaked with the weight of bags of money. In the armoury, between standards and wild beasts' heads, could be seen weapons of every age and every nation, from the slings of the Amalekites and the javelins of the Garamantes to the short swords of the Saracens and Norman coats of mail. The chief spit in the kitchen could roast an ox; the chapel was as splendid as a king's oratory. There was even, in a secluded corner, a Roman vapour-bath; but the good lord abstained from using it, considering it a practice of the heathen.

Wrapped always in a mantle of fox skins, he walked about his castle, administering justice to his vassals and setting the disputes of his neighbours at rest. In winter he watched the snowflakes falling or had stories read to him. With the first fine days he rode out on his mule along the by-ways, beside the greening corn, and chatted with the peasants, to whom he gave advice. After many adventures he had taken a lady of high lineage as his wife.

Very white of skin she was, a little proud and serious. The horns of her coif brushed against the door lintel, and the train of her dress trailed three paces behind her. Her household was ordered like the inside of a monastery; every morning she gave out the tasks to the servants, inspected the preserves and unguents, span at her distaff or embroidered altar-cloths. By dint of prayer to God a son was born to her.

Then there were great rejoicings and a banquet which lasted three days and four nights, with the illumination of torches, the sound of harps, and strewing of green branches. They ate of the rarest spices, and fowls as large as sheep; a dwarf came out of a pasty, to amuse the guests; and as the throng was always increasing and the bowls would go round no longer, they were obliged to drink out of horns and helmets.

The lady who had just been made a mother was not present at this cheer. She stayed quietly in her bed. Waking one evening, she saw as it were a shadow moving under a ray of the moon which came through the window. It was an old man in a frieze gown, with a chaplet at his side, a wallet on his shoulder, and all the semblance of a hermit. He came towards her pillow and said to her, without opening his lips:

"Rejoice, O mother, thy son shall be a saint!"

She was just going to cry out, but he glided over the streak of moonlight, rose gently into the air and vanished. The songs of the banqueters broke out louder. She heard angels' voices; and her head fell back on the pillow, over which, framed with garnets, hung a martyr's bone.

Next morning all the servants were questioned and said they had seen no hermit. Whether it were a dream or reality, it must have been a communication from Heaven; but she was careful not to speak of it, fearing she might be taxed with pride.

The guests went off at morning twilight, and Julian's father was outside the postern gate, to which he had just escorted the last to go, when suddenly a beggar rose before him in the mist. He was a gipsy, with a plaited beard and silver rings on his arms, and fiery eyes. With an air of inspiration he stammered these disjointed words:

"Ah, ah! thy son! Blood in plenty! . . . Fame in plenty! . . . Blest always—the family of an emperor!"

And stooping to pick up his alms he was lost in the grass and disappeared.

The good castellan looked right and left, and called with all his might. No one! The wind blew shrill; the mists of morning flew away.

He put down this vision to a weary head, from having slept too little. "If I speak of it they will make a jest of me," he said to himself. Yet the glories destined to his son dazzled him, although the promise was not clear and he doubted even whether he had heard it.

The husband and wife each kept their secret. But they cherished their child, both of them, with an equal love; and, reverencing him as marked out by God, had an infinite care for his

person. His cot was stuffed with the finest
down; a lamp shaped like a dove burned con-
tinually above it, three nurses rocked him;
and well swaddled in his clothes, with his rosy
looks and blue eyes, a brocade cloak and a
cap set with pearls, he looked a little Jesus.
He teethed without crying at any time.

When he was seven his mother taught him
to sing. To make him brave his father lifted
him on to a big horse. The child smiled with
pleasure and before long knew all about
chargers.

A learned old monk taught him Holy Writ,
the Arabic way of counting, the Latin letters,
and how to make dainty pictures on vellum.
They worked together high up in a turret away
from all noise. The lesson over, they came
down into the garden and studied the flowers,
pausing at every step.

Sometimes a string of laden beasts was seen
passing below in the valley, led by a man on
foot dressed in the Eastern way. The castellan, recognizing him for a merchant, would
send a servant out to him, and the stranger,
taking heart, would turn out of his road. He
would be brought into the parlour, where he
drew out of his coffers strips of velvet and silk,

jewels, perfumes, and curious things of unknown use; after which the worthy man went
off, having taken a great profit and suffered no
violence. At other times a band of pilgrims
would come knocking at the gate. Their drag-
gled garments steamed before the fire; and
when they had been well fed they told the story
of their travels: wanderings on shipboard over
foamy seas, journeyings afoot in burning sands,
the furious rage of paynims, the caves of Syria,
the Manger and the Sepulchre. Then they
would give the young lord scallop-shells from
their cloaks.

Often the castellan feasted his old
companions-at-arms. While they drank they
called to mind their wars and the storming of
fortresses, with the crash of warlike engines
and the prodigious wounds. Julian listened
to them and uttered cries; and his father had
no doubt, then, that he would be a conqueror
one day. Yet at evening, coming from the
Angelus, as he passed between the bending
rows of poor, he dipped in his purse with such
modesty and so noble a mien that his mother
thought surely to see him an archbishop in his
time.

His place in chapel was by the side of his

parents, and however long the offices might be he stayed kneeling at his stool, with his cap on the floor and his hands clasped in prayer.

One day, while mass was being said, he raised his head and saw a little white mouse coming out of a hole in the wall. It trotted along the first pace of the altar, and after making two or three turns to right and left fled by the way it had come. Next Sunday he was troubled by the thought that he might see it again. It did come back; and then every Sunday he watched for it, was troubled, seized with hatred for it, and determined to get rid of the mouse.

So, having shut the door and sprinkled some cake-crumbs along the altar steps, he took post in front of the hole with a little stick in his hand.

After a very long time a small pink nose appeared, and then the entire mouse. He struck a light blow, and stood lost in amazement at this tiny body which did not stir again. A drop of blood spotted the pavement. Julian wiped it off rapidly with his sleeve, threw the mouse away, and did not say a word to anyone.

There were all kinds of little birds which pecked at the seeds in the garden. Julian had the thought of putting peas into a hollow reed.

When he heard the sound of chirruping in a tree he came up softly, lifted his pipe, and blew out his cheeks; and the little creatures rained down in such abundance on his shoulders that he could not help laughing in delight at his trick.

One morning, as he was going back along the curtain wall, he saw a fat pigeon on the top of the rampart, preening itself in the sun. Julian stopped to look at it, and as there was a breach in this part of the wall a fragment of stone lay ready to his hand. He swung his arm, and the stone brought down the bird, which fell like a lump into the moat.

He dashed down after it, tearing himself in the briars and scouring everywhere, nimbler than a young dog. The pigeon, its wings broken, hung quivering in the boughs of a privet. The obstinate life in it annoyed the child. He began to throttle it, and the bird's convulsions made his heart beat, filled him with a savage, passionate delight. When it stiffened for the last time he felt that he would swoon.

At supper in the evening his father declared that it was time for him to learn the art of venery, and he went to look for an old manuscript which contained, in questions and an-

swers, the whole pastime of the chase. A
master explained in it to his pupil the craft of
breaking-in dogs, taming falcons, and setting
snares; how to know the stag by his droppings,
the fox by his footmarks, the wolf by his
scratchings of the ground; the right way to dis-
cern their tracks, the manner of starting them,
the usual places of their lairs, the most favour-
able winds, and a list of all the calls and the
rules for the quarry.

When Julian could repeat all this by heart his
father gathered a pack of hounds for him.

The first to catch the eye were twenty-four
greyhounds from Barbary, swifter than gazelles, but prone to get out of hand; and then
seventeen couples of Breton hounds, with red
coats and white spots, unshakable in control,
deep-chested, loud to bay. To face the wild
boar and its dangerous redoublings there were
forty boarhounds, as shaggy as bears. Mastiffs from Tartary nearly as tall as asses and
flame-coloured, with broad backs and straight
legs, were assigned to hunt the aurochs. The
black coats of the spaniels shone like satin, and
the yapping of the talbots matched the chant-
ing of the beagles. In a yard by themselves,
tossing their chains and rolling their eyes,

growled eight Alain dogs, fearsome animals that fly at the belly of a horseman and have no dread of lions.

All of them ate wheaten bread, drank out of stone troughs, and bore sonorous names.

The falconry, maybe, was choicer even than the pack; for by dint of money the good lord had secured tiercelets of the Caucasus, sakers from Babylonia, gerfalcons of Germany, and peregrines taken on the cliffs at the edge of cold seas in far quarters of the world. They were housed in a big shed roofed with thatch, and fastened to the perching-bar in a row according to their size, with a strip of turf before them where they were placed from time to time to unstiffen their limbs.

Purse-nets, hooks, wolf-traps, and engines of every kind were artfully made.

Often they took out setters into the country, who quickly came to a point. Then huntsmen, advancing step by step, cautiously spread a huge net over their motionless bodies. At a word of command they barked; quails took wing; and the ladies of the neighbourhood who had been bidden with their husbands, the children, the handmaids, the whole company darted on the birds and easily caught them.

At other times they would beat drums to start the hares; foxes fell into pits, or a trap would spring and take hold of a wolf's paw.

But Julian spurned these handy devices. He preferred to hunt far away from the rest with his horse and his falcon. It was almost always a great Scythian tartaret, white as snow. Its leathern hood was topped with a plume, bells of gold quivered on its blue feet; and it stood firmly in its master's arm while the horse galloped and the plains unrolled below. Julian, freeing the jesses, would suddenly let it go; the daring bird rose straight as an arrow into the sky; and you saw two specks, one larger and one smaller, circle, meet, and then vanish in the high blue spaces. The falcon soon came down, tearing a quarry, and returned to perch on the gauntlet with its wings a-quiver.

In that way Julian flew his falcons at the heron, the kite, the crow, and the vulture.

He loved to blow his horn and follow his hounds as they coursed along the sloping hills, jumped the streams, and climbed to the woods again; and when the stag began groaning under their bites he felled it cleverly, and was delighted by the fury of the mastiffs as they devoured it, hewn in pieces on its reeking hide.

On misty days he went down into a marsh to ambush the geese, otters, and wild duck.

Three squires waited for him from dawn at the foot of the steps, and though the old monk might lean out of his window and make signs to call him back Julian would not turn. He went out in the heat of the sun, under the rain, and amidst storms, drinking water from the springs out of his hand, munching wild apples as he trotted along, and resting under an oak if he were tired; and he came in at midnight covered in blood and mire, with thorns in his hair and the odour of the wild beasts hanging round him. He became as one of them. When his mother kissed him he took her embrace coldly, and seemed to be dreaming of deep things.

He slew bears with strokes of his knife, bulls with the axe, and wild boars with the pike; and once, even, defended himself with nothing but a stick against wolves that were gnawing corpses at the foot of a gibbet.

One winter morning he started in full trim before dawn, with a cross-bow on his shoulder and a quiver of arrows at his saddle-bow.

His Danish jennet, followed by two bassets, made the earth ring under its even tread. Drops of rime stuck to his cloak, and a fierce breeze blew. The sky lightened at one side, and in the pale twilight he saw rabbits hopping at the edge of their burrows. The two bassets dashed for them at once, jumping hither and thither as they broke their backs.

Soon after he entered a wood. At the end of a branch a grouse, numbed by the cold, slept with its head under its wing. With a back-stroke of his sword Julian cut off its two feet, and without stopping to pick it up went on his way.

Three hours later he found himself on the top of a mountain, which was so high that the sky seemed almost black. A rock like a long wall sloped away in front of him, cresting a precipice; and at the farther end of it two wild goats were looking down into the chasm. Not having his arrows at hand—he had left his horse behind—he thought he would go right down upon the goats; and stooping double, barefoot, he reached the first of them at last and plunged his dagger under its ribs. The other was seized with panic and jumped into the abyss. Julian leaped to strike it, and his right foot slipping, fell across the body of the first, with his face hanging over the gulf and arms flung wide.

He came down into the plain again and fol-

lowed a line of willows bordering a river.
Cranes, flying very low, passed overhead from
time to time. Julian brought them down with
his whip, not missing one.

Meanwhile the air had grown warmer and
melted the rime; there were broad wreaths of
vapour floating, and the sun appeared. Far
off he saw a still lake glistening like a sheet of
lead. In the middle of it was an animal
which Julian did not know, a black-headed
beaver. In spite of the distance he killed it
with an arrow, and was vexed not to be able to
carry off its skin.

Then he went on down an avenue of great
trees, whose tops made a kind of triumphal
arch at the entrance of a forest. A roebuck
bounded out of a thicket, a fallow deer showed
itself at a crossing, a badger came out of a
hole, a peacock spread its tail on the grass;
and when he had slain them all more roebuck,
deer, badgers, peacocks and blackbirds, jays,
polecats, foxes, hedgehogs, lynxes—an endless
company of beasts—appeared and grew more
numerous at every step. Tremblingly they circled round him, with gentle supplicating looks.
But Julian did not tire of killing, by turns bending his cross-bow, unsheathing his long sword,
and thrusting with his short, thinking of noth-

ing, with no memory of anything at all. Only the fact of his existence told him that for an indefinite time he had been hunting in some vague country, where all happened with the ease of dreams. An extraordinary sight brought him to a halt. A valley shaped like an arena was filled with stags, who crowded close together warming each other with their breath, which could be seen steaming in the mist.

The prospect of a slaughter like this for a minute or two took Julian's breath away for pleasure. Then he dismounted, rolled up his sleeves, and began to shoot.

At the whistle of the first arrow all the stags turned their heads at once. Hollows opened in the mass, plaintive cries rose, and a great stir shook the herd.

The brim of the valley was too high to climb. They leaped about in this enclosure, trying to escape. Julian aimed and shot, and the arrows fell like rain shafts in a thunder-storm. The maddened stags fought, reared, and climbed on each other's backs; and the bodies and entangled antlers made a broad mound which crumbled and changed.

At last they died, stretched on the sand, their nostrils frothing, entrails bursting, and

bellies slowly ceasing to heave. Then all was
motionless. Night was close at hand; and behind the woods, in the interspaces of the
boughs, the sky was red as a sheet of blood.

Julian leant back against a tree, and gazed
with staring eyes at the enormous massacre; he
could not think how it had been done.

Then across the valley, at the edge of the
forest, he saw a stag with its hind and its
fawn.

The stag was black and hugely tall; it carried sixteen points and a white beard. The
hind, pale yellow like a dead leaf, was grazing;
and the spotted fawn, without hindering her
movements, pulled at her dugs.

Once more the cross-bow sang. The fawn
was killed on the spot. Then its mother,
looking skywards, bellowed with a deep, heart-
breaking, human cry. In exasperation Julian
stretched her on the ground with a shot full in
the breast.

The great stag had seen it, and made a
bound. Julian shot his last arrow at him. It
hit the stag in the forehead and stuck fast
there.

The great stag did not seem to feel it; strid-
ing over the dead bodies, he came on and on,
in act to charge and disembowel him; and

Julian retreated in unspeakable terror. The
monstrous creature stopped, and with flaming
eyes, as solemn as a patriarch or judge, said
three times, while a bell tinkled in the distance:

"Accurst! accurst! accurst! one day, fero-
cious heart, thou shalt murder thy father and
thy mother!"

The stag's knees bent, his eyes closed gently,
and he died.

Julian was thunderstruck, and then suddenly
felt crushed with fatigue; disgust and boundless sadness came over him. He buried his
face in his hands and wept for a long time.

His horse was lost, his dogs had left him;
the solitude which folded round him seemed
looming with vague dangers. Seized with
alarm, he struck across country, and choosing
a path at random found himself almost immediately at the castle-gate.

He could not sleep at night. By the flick-
ering of the hanging lamps he always saw the
great black stag. The creature's prophecy besieged him, and he fought against it. "No!
no! no! it cannot be that I should kill them!"
And then he mused: "Yet if I should wish to
kill?" and he was afraid that the Devil might
inspire him with the wish.

For three months his mother prayed in an-

guish by his pillow, and his father walked to
and fro along the corridors with groans. He
sent for the most famous master physicians,
who prescribed quantities of drugs. Julian's
malady, they said, was caused by a noxious
wind, or by a love-desire. But the young man,
in answer to all questions, shook his head.

His strength came back to him, and they
took him out to walk in the courtyard, the old
monk and the good lord each propping him
with an arm.

When he had recovered altogether he ob-
stinately refused to hunt. His father, hoping to cheer him, made him a present of a
great Saracen sword. It was in a stand of
arms, at the top of a pillar, and a ladder was
needed to reach it. Julian went up. The
sword was too heavy and slipped from his
fingers, and in the fall grazed the worthy lord
so close as to cut his mantle; Julian thought
he had killed his father, and fainted away.

From that moment he dreaded weapons.
The sight of a bare blade made him turn pale.
This weakness was a sorrow to his family, and
at last the old monk, in the name of God, of
honour, and his ancestors, bade him take up the
exercises of his gentle birth again.

The squires amused themselves daily at

practising with the javelin. Julian very
quickly excelled in this; he could throw his
javelin into the neck of a bottle, break the
teeth of a weather-vane, and hit the nails on
a door a hundred paces off.

One summer evening, at the hour when
things grow indistinct in the dusk, he was under the trellis in the garden and saw right at
the end of it two white wings fluttering by the
top of its supports. He made sure it was a
stork, and threw his javelin. A piercing cry
rang out.

It was his mother, whose bonnet with long
flaps stayed pinned to the wall.

Julian fled from the castle and was seen
there no more.

II

He took service with a passing troop of ad-
venturers and knew hunger and thirst, fevers
and vermin. He grew accustomed to the din
of mellays and the sight of dying men. The
wind tanned his skin. His limbs hardened
under the clasp of armour; and as he was
very strong, valiant, temperate, and wary he
won the command of a company with ease.

When a battle opened he swept on his soldiers with a great flourish of his sword. He

scaled the walls of citadels with a knotted rope
at night, swinging in the blasts, while sparks
of Greek fire stuck to his cuirass and boiling
resin and molten lead hissed from the battlements. Often a stone crashed and shivered
his buckler. Bridges overladen with men gave
way under him. Swinging his battle-axe to and
fro, he got rid of fourteen horsemen. In the
lists he overcame all challengers. More than
a score of times he was left for dead.

Thanks to the favour of Heaven he always
came out safely, for he protected clerks, or-
phans, widows, and, most of all, old men.
When he saw one of them walking in front of
him he called out to see his face, as though he
were afraid of killing him by mistake.

Runaway slaves, peasants in revolt, fortune-
less bastards, and venturous men of all sorts
flocked under his banner, and he made an army
of his own.

It grew, and he became famous. The
world sought him out. He succoured in turn
the Dauphin of France and the King of England, the Templars of Jerusalem, the Surena
of the Parthians, the Negus of Abyssinia, and
the Emperor of Calicut. He fought against
Scandinavians covered with fish-scales, negroes
with bucklers of hippopotamus hide, mounted

on red asses, and gold-coloured Indians flour-
ishing broadswords brighter than mirrors
above their diadems. He subdued the Trog-
lodytes and the Anthropophages. He went
through such burning regions that the hair on
the head caught fire of itself, like torches, in
the sun's heat; through others so freezing
that the arms snapped from the body and fell
to the ground; and countries where there was
so much mist that you walked surrounded by
phantoms.

Republics in distress consulted him, and
in colloquies with ambassadors he gained
unhoped-for terms. If a monarch behaved
too badly Julian was quickly on the spot and
took him to task. He set free peoples and de-
livered queens immured in towers. He it was,
no other, who slew the viper of Milan and the
dragon of Oberbirbach.

Now the Emperor of Occitania, having tri-
umphed over the Spanish Moslems, had taken
the sister of the Caliph of Cordova as his con-
cubine, and by her he had a daughter whom
he had brought up to be a Christian. But the
Caliph, feigning a wish to be converted, came
to return his visit with a numerous escort, put
all his garrison to the sword, and threw him

into an underground dungeon, where he used him cruelly to extort his treasure.

Julian hastened to his aid, destroyed the army of the infidels, besieged the town, killed the Caliph, cut off his head, and threw it over the ramparts like a ball. Then he drew the emperor out of prison and set him on his throne again, in the presence of all his court.

To requite this great service the emperor presented him with basketfuls of money; Julian would have none of it. Thinking that he wanted more, he offered him three-quarters of his wealth, and was refused again; then the half of his kingdom; Julian thanked him and declined. The emperor was in tears of distress, seeing no way to show his gratitude, when he tapped his forehead and whispered in a courtier's ear; the curtains of a tapestry lifted and a maiden appeared.

Her large dark eyes gleamed like two gentle lamps; her lips were parted in a winning smile. The ringlets of her hair caught in the jewels of a half-opened robe, and under the transparent tunic the young lines of her body could be guessed. She was slim of figure, all daintiness and softness.

Julian was dazzled with love, the more because he had lived in great chastity till then.

So he took the emperor's daughter in marriage, with a castle that she held from her mother; and when the wedding was over he and his host parted, after a long exchange of courtesies.

It was a palace of white marble, in the Moorish fashion, built on a promontory in a grove of orange-trees. Terraces of flowers sloped to the edge of a bay, where there were pink shells that crackled underfoot. Behind the castle stretched a forest in the shape of a fan. The sky was blue unceasingly, and the trees waved by turns under the sea breeze and the wind from the mountains, which closed the horizon far away.

The rooms were full of shadow, but drew light from their incrusted walls. High columns, slender as reeds, supported their domed vaults, which were embossed in relief to imitate the stalactites in caves. There were fountains in the greater rooms, mosaics in the courts, festooned partitions, delicacies of architecture beyond number, and everywhere so deep a silence that one heard the rustle of a scarf or the echo of a sigh.

Julian made war no longer. He rested with

a quiet people round him, and every day a
crowd passed before him, making obeisances
and kissing hands in the Eastern style.

In his purple dress he would stay leaning
in the embrasure of a window, recalling his
hunts of former days; and he would have liked
to scour the desert after gazelles and ostriches,
hide among the bamboos to wait for leopards,
traverse forests full of rhinoceroses, climb the
most inaccessible mountain-tops to take better
aim at eagles, and fight with white bears on ice-
bergs in the sea.

Sometimes, in dreams, he saw himself like
our father Adam in the midst of Paradise,
among all the beasts. He stretched out his
arm against them, and they died; or else,
again, they defiled before him, two by two according to their size, from the elephants and
lions to the ermines and the ducks, as on the
day when they entered Noah's ark. From the
shadow of a cave he rained darts on them
which never missed; other animals appeared;
there was no end to them, and he woke with
his eyes rolling wildly.

Among his friends there were princes who
invited him to hunt. He always refused, thinking that by a penance of this kind he would turn
aside his curse, for it seemed to him that the

slaughter of animals would decide the fate of his father and mother. But it was a grief to him not to see his parents, and his other secret desire became impossible to bear.

His wife sent for jugglers and dancers to amuse him. She went out with him into the country in an open litter; and at other times they would lie in a boat and watch, over the side, the fish roaming in water as clear as the sky. Often she threw flowers in his face, or crouching at his feet drew music from a three-stringed mandolin; and then, laying her clasped hands on his shoulder, said timidly, "What ails thee then, dear lord?"

He did not answer, or broke into sobs. At last, one day, he confessed his horrible thought.

She fought against it, arguing very well. His father and mother, most likely, were already dead; but if he ever saw them again what chance or purpose could lead him to this abominable deed? His fear was causeless, then, and he should return to the hunt.

Julian smiled as he listened to her, but could not make up his mind to fulfil his desire.

One August evening they were in their chamber, she being just in bed and he kneeling down to pray, when he heard a fox barking, and then some light footfalls under the window. He caught a glimpse, in the dusk, of what seemed to be the shapes of animals. The temptation was too strong, and he took down his quiver.

She showed surprise.

"I do it to obey you," he said; "I shall be back at sunrise." Still, she was afraid of a disastrous venture.

He reassured her and went out, surprised at her inconsistent mood.

Soon afterwards a page came in to say that two strangers, as they could not see the absent lord, were asking instantly to see his lady.

And soon there entered the room an old man and an old woman, bowed and dusty, dressed in rough linen, each leaning on a staff.

Taking courage, they said that they were bringing Julian news of his parents. She leaned out of bed to listen.

But, having first exchanged a look, they asked her if he was still fond of them, and if he spoke of them at times.

"Ah, yes!" she said.

"Well, we are they!" they cried, and, being very weary and spent with fatigue, sat down.

The young wife felt no assurance that her husband was their son, but they proved it by describing some particular marks on his skin.

Then she leaped out of bed, called the page, and a repast was served to them.

They could scarcely eat, though they were very hungry; she observed, aside, how their bony hands trembled as they grasped the cups. They asked countless questions about Julian, and she answered all, but took care not to speak of the ghastly fancy in which they were concerned.

After waiting in vain for his return they had left their castle, and they had been travelling for several years after vague clues, without losing hope. So much money had been swallowed up by river-tolls and inns, the dues of princes and demands of thieves that their purse was emptied to the bottom, and now they begged their way. But what of that, when they would soon embrace their son? They extolled his happiness to have so fair a wife, and could not have enough of watching her and kissing her.

They were much astonished by the richness of the room, and the old man, after examining its walls, asked why the Emperor of Occitania's coat-of-arms was there.

"He is my father," she replied.

At that he started, remembering the gipsy's prophecy, while the old woman thought of the hermit's words. Doubtless their son's glory was but the dawn of an eternal splendour; and they both sat open-mouthed under the light of the great candlestick upon the table.

They must have been very handsome in their youth. The mother had kept all her hair, and its fine plaits hung to the bottom of her cheeks like drifts of snow. The father, with his height and his great beard, was like a statue in a church.

Julian's wife persuaded them not to wait for him. With her own hands she placed them in her bed, then shut the window, and they went to sleep. Daybreak was near, and little birds were beginning to sing outside.

Julian had crossed the park and walked through the forest with a springing step, enjoying the soft turf and mild night air. Shadows fell from the trees across the moss. From time to time the moonlight made white patches in the drives and he hesitated to go forward, thinking he saw a pool; or, again, the surface of the still ponds would itself be lost in the colour of the grass. There was a deep silence everywhere, and he found no trace of the animals which a few minutes earlier had been straying round his castle.

The wood thickened and grew profoundly dark. Puffs of warm air went by him, with

relaxing scents. His feet sank among dead
leaves, and he leaned against an oak to breathe
a little.

Suddenly, from behind his back, a darker
mass leaped out. It was a wild boar. Julian
had no time to snatch his bow, and was as
vexed as though it was a disaster.

Then, when he had left the wood, he saw
a wolf stealing along a hedge. Julian sent an
arrow after it. The wolf paused, turned
round to look at him, and went on again. It
trotted on, always at the same distance, stopping from time to time, and taking flight again
as soon as Julian aimed.

In this way Julian went over an endless plain
and a tract of sand-hills, and came out upon
high ground which looked over a great breadth
of country. Flat stones lay scattered on it
from ruined vaults all round. His feet stumbled on dead bones, and in places there were
worm-eaten crosses leaning mournfully askew.
But forms stirred in the dim shadow of the
tombs; and hyenas rose out of them, scared
and panting. Their hoofs clattered on the
pave-stones as they came up to Julian, sniffing
at him and showing their gums with a yawn.
When he drew his sword they went off at once
in all directions, with a headlong, limping gal-

lop which lasted till they vanished in the distance under a cloud of dust.

An hour later he met a savage bull in a ravine, lowering its horns and ploughing the sand up with its foot. Julian thrust with his lance at it under the dew-lap. The lance was shivered, as though the animal were made of bronze; he closed his eyes, expecting to be killed. When he reopened them the bull had disappeared.

Then his heart sank for shame. A higher power was bringing his strength to nought, and he went back into the forest to regain his home.

The forest was tangled with creepers; and as he was cutting them with his sword a marten slipped sharply between his legs, a panther made a bound over his shoulder, and a snake wound its way up an ash tree. A huge jackdaw looked down at Julian out of its leaves, and on every side among the branches appeared a multitude of great sparks, as though the firmament had showered all its stars into the forest. They were eyes of animals—wild cats, squirrels, owls, parrots, monkeys.

Julian darted his arrows at them; the feathered shafts settled on the leaves like white butterflies. He threw stones at them, and the stones fell back without touching anything. He cursed, wanted to fight, shouted imprecations, and choked with rage.

And all the animals which he had been hunting appeared again and made a narrow circle round him. Some sat upon their haunches, others stood erect. He was rooted in the middle, frozen with terror, and impotent to move at all. With a supreme effort of will he took a step; the creatures on the branches spread their wings, those on the ground stretched their limbs, and all went on with him.

The hyenas walked in front, the wolf and the boar behind. The bull was on his right, swaying its head, while on his left the serpent wound through the grass and the panther arched its back and advanced with long, velvet-footed strides. He walked as slowly as he could to avoid irritating them; and as he went he saw porcupines, foxes, vipers, jackals, and bears come out of the dense undergrowth.

Julian began to run; they ran too. The serpent hissed, and the stinking creatures slavered. The wild boar's tusks prodded his heels, and the wolf rubbed the palms of his hands with his hairy muzzle. The monkeys pinched him and made faces, and the marten rolled over his feet. A bear swung its paw back and knocked his hat off, and the panther, which had been carrying an arrow in its mouth, let it fall in disdain.

Their sly movements gave peeps of irony. As they watched him out of the corner of their eyes they seemed to be meditating a plan of revenge; while he, deafened by the buzzing insects, lashed by the birds' tails, and smothered by the breath of the animals, walked with arms outstretched and eyes shut like a blind man, without even having strength to cry for mercy.

A cock-crow rang in the air, and others answered. It was day, and he recognized his palace roof beyond the orange-trees.

Then at the edge of a field he saw, three paces off him, some red partridges fluttering in the stubble. He unfastened his cloak and threw it over them as a net. When he uncovered them he found but one, long dead and rotten.

This deception infuriated him more than all the others. His thirst to kill swept over him again, and for want of beasts he would gladly have slain men.

He climbed the three terraces and burst open the door with a blow of his fist; but when he reached the staircase his heart unbent at the thought of his dear wife. She was asleep, doubtless, and he would take her by surprise.

He drew off his sandals, turned the lock gently, and went in.

The pale dawn came dimly through the leaded window-panes. Julian's feet caught in clothes lying on the floor; a little farther, and he knocked against a buffet still laden with plate. "Her supper, doubtless," he said to himself, and went on towards the bed, which he could not see in the darkness at the end of the room. He came close, and to kiss his wife bent down over the pillow where the two heads were lying side by side. Then he felt the touch of a beard against his mouth.

He drew back, thinking he was going mad, but came near the bed again, and as he felt about with his fingers they encountered long tresses of hair. To convince himself that he was wrong he passed his hand again slowly over the pillow. It was really a beard this time, and a man—a man lying with his wife!

In a fit of boundless fury he leaped on them, striking with his dagger; he stamped and foamed, roaring like a wild beast. Then he stopped. The dead folk, pierced to the heart, had not so much as stirred. He listened closely to their dying groans, which almost kept time together; and as they grew feebler

another, in the far distance, took them up.
Vague at first, this plaintive, long-drawn voice
came nearer, swelled, rang cruelly; and he recognized in terror the belling of the great black
stag.

And as he turned round he thought he saw
his wife's ghost framed in the doorway, with
a light in her hand.

The noise of the murder had drawn her
there. In one wide glance she grasped it all,
and fled in horror, dropping her torch. He
picked it up.

His father and mother lay before him,
stretched on their backs, with breasts pierced
through; and their faces, in a gentle majesty,
looked as though they were keeping a secret
for ever. Splashes and pools of blood showed
on their white skin, over the bed-clothes and
the floor, and trickled down an ivory crucifix
in the alcove. The scarlet reflection from the
window, which the sun was striking, lit up
these red patches and cast others, more numerous still, all round the room. Julian walked
towards the two dead figures, saying to himself, and struggling to believe, that this thing
could not be and that he was deceived by an
error—by one of those resemblances which
nothing can explain. Finally he bent down a

little to look close at the old man, and saw between the unshut eyelids a glazed eye which scorched him like fire. Then he went to the other side of the couch where the other body lay, its white hair hiding part of the face. Julian passed his fingers under the plaits and lifted the head; and holding it at arm's length with one hand, while in the other he held up the torch, he looked at it. Drops of blood were oozing from the mattress and falling one by one upon the floor.

At the end of the day he came into his wife's presence; and in a voice not his own bade her first of all not to answer him, come near him, or even look at him. Under pain of damnation she must follow all his orders, which would not be gainsaid.

The funerals must be carried out according to injunctions which he had left in writing, on a prie-dieu in the chamber of the dead. He ceded to her his palace, his vassals, and all his possessions, not excepting even his clothes or his sandals, which would be found at the head of the stairs.

She had obeyed God's will in making the occasion of his crime, and she must pray for his soul, since from that day he ceased to exist.

The dead were sumptuously buried in an abbey church at three days' journey from the castle. A monk in shrouded hood followed the procession at a distance from the others, and no one dared to speak to him. He remained while the mass lasted, lying flat in the middle of the porch, with his arms making the form of a cross and his forehead in the dust.

After the burial he was seen to take the road leading to the mountains. He turned to look round several times, and finally disappeared.

III

He went onwards, begging his way throughout the world.

He held out his hand to the riders on the high-roads and bent his knee when he approached the reapers. Or he would stand motionless before the gates of courtyards, and his face was so sad that he was never refused alms.

In a spirit of humbleness he would tell his story; and then all fled from him, making the sign of the cross. In the villages which he had passed through before, the people, as soon as they recognized him, shut their doors, shouted abuse at him, threw stones at him.

The most charitable of them placed a bowl on their window-sills and then closed the shutters so as not to see him.

Being repulsed everywhere, he shunned mankind, and fed on roots, plants, wayside fruit, and shell-fish which he gathered along the beaches.

Sometimes, at the turn of a hillside, he saw a jumble of crowded roofs under his eyes, with stone spires, bridges, towers, and a network of dark streets, from which a ceaseless hum rose up to him. A need to mingle with the life of others would draw him down into the town. But the brutal look in their faces, their noisy crafts and callous words, made his heart freeze. On festal days, when the great cathedral bells tuned the whole populace to joy from daybreak, he watched the folk issuing from their houses, and the dancing in public spaces, the beer fountains at the crossways, the damask hung before the lodgings of princes; and then at evening, through the lower windows, the long family tables where grandparents dandled little children on their knees. Sobs choked him, and he turned away towards the country.

He had thrills of love as he gazed at young

horses in the meadows, birds in their nests, and insects on the flowers; all, at his approach, ran farther off, hid in terror, or flew swiftly away.

He sought deserted places. But the wind grated on his ear like the rattle of a death-agony; the dew-drops falling to the ground brought other, heavier drops to mind. Every evening the sun tinged the clouds blood-red, and each night the murder of his parents began again in dreams.

He made himself a hair shirt with iron spikes, and climbed on his knees up every hill which had a chapel at the top. But his piti-less thought dimmed the radiance of the shrines, and stung him even in his acts of morti-fication. He did not rebel against God for having brought the deed upon him, and yet the idea that he could have done it made him despair.

His own person filled him with such hor-ror that in the hope of release he risked it among dangers. He saved the paralysed from fires and children from the bottom of chasms. The abyss cast him up; the flames spared him.

Time brought no relief to his suffering. It became intolerable, and he resolved to die.

And one day when he was by a spring, leaning over it to judge the water's depth, he saw opposite him on a sudden an emaciated old man, with a white beard and a look so dolorous that Julian could not keep back his tears. The other wept also. Without recognizing him exactly, Julian had a confused memory of a face like his. He uttered a cry; it was his father; and he thought no more of killing himself.

So with the burden of his recollections he travelled many lands, and came one day to a river, which, owing to its violence and a great stretch of slime along its banks, was dangerous to cross. No one for a long time had dared to make the passage.

An old boat, whose stern had been embedded, lifted its prow among the reeds. Julian examined it and found a pair of oars; and the thought came to him that he might use his life in the service of others.

He began by making a sort of roadway on the bank to lead down to the channel of the river; and he broke his nails in moving enormous stones, propped them against his waist to carry them, slipped in the mud and sank there, and nearly perished several times. Then he repaired the boat with pieces of wreckage, and made a hut for himself out of clay and tree-trunks.

The ferry came to be heard of and travellers appeared. They waved flags and hailed him from the other side, and Julian at once jumped into his boat. It was very heavy, and they overweighted it with baggage and loads of all kinds, without counting the beasts of burden, who made the crowding worse by kicking in alarm. He asked nothing for his labour; some of the passengers gave him remnants of food out of their wallets or worn-out clothes which they had no more use for. The brutal ones shouted blasphemies. Julian reproved them gently, and they retorted with abuse. He was content to bless them.

A little table, a stool, a bed of dry leaves, and three clay cups—that was the whole of his furniture. Two holes in the wall served for windows. On one side barren plains stretched away out of view, dotted with pale meres here and there; and in front of him the great river rolled its greenish waters. In spring the damp soil breathed an odour of decay. Then came a riotous wind that lifted the dust and whirled it. It found its way in everywhere, muddying the water and grating in the mouth. A little later there were clouds of mosquitoes, which pinged and pricked without ceasing day and night. And then came on appalling frosts which turned everything to the hardness of stone and roused a wild craving to eat meat.

Months glided by when Julian did not see a soul. Often he closed his eyes and tried to revive his youth in memory. The courtyard of a castle would rise before him, with greyhounds on a flight of steps, grooms in the armoury, and a fair-haired boy under a vine trellis between an old man dressed in furs and a lady wearing a great coif. Suddenly, the two corpses were there. He threw himself face downwards on his bed and kept murmuring with tears:

"Ah, poor father! Poor mother, poor mother!"—and fell into a drowsiness through which the mournful visions still went on.

When he was asleep one night he thought he heard someone calling him. He strained his ears and made out nothing except the roar of the water.

But the same voice cried again: "Julian!"

It came from the other bank, which amazed him, considering the breadth of the river.

A third time he was hailed: "Julian!"

And the loud voice had the tone of a church bell.

Julian lit his lantern and went out of the
hovel. A wild hurricane was sweeping through
the night. There was an intense darkness,
pierced now and then by the whiteness of the
leaping waves.

After a moment's hesitation Julian unfastened his moorings. The water instantly became calm, and the boat glided over it to the
other bank, where a man stood waiting.

He was wrapped in a tattered cloth and his
face was like a plaster mask, with eyes redder
than coals. Holding the lantern to him, Julian saw that he was covered with a hideous
leprosy; yet there was something of a royal
majesty in his posture.

As soon as he entered the boat it sank pro-
digiously, overwhelmed by his weight. It
rose again with a shake, and Julian began to
row.

At every stroke the surf tossed the boat up
by its bows. The water, blacker than ink, ran
furiously against the planks on both sides. It
hollowed into gulfs and rose into mountains,
which the boat leaped over, only to fall back
into the depths, where it spun round at the
mercy of the wind.

Julian bent low, stretched his arms out, and
propping himself against his feet swung back

with a twist to get more power. The hail lashed his hands, the rain streamed down his back, he could not breathe in the fierce wind, and stopped. Then the boat drifted and was carried away. But feeling that there was a great matter at stake, an order which might not be disobeyed, he took up the oars again, and the clacking of the thole-pins cut through the stormy clamour.

The little lantern burned in front of him. Birds hid it from time to time as they fluttered by. But he always saw the eyes of the Leper, who stood, motionless as a pillar, at the stern.

It went on long, very long.

When at last they had entered the hovel Julian shut the door; and he saw the Leper sitting on the stool. The kind of shroud which covered him had fallen to his hips; and his shoulders, chest, and wizened arms were hardly to be seen for the scaly pustules which coated them. Immense wrinkles furrowed his brow. He had a hole in place of a nose, like a skeleton, and his bluish lips exhaled a breath as thick as fog, and nauseous.

"I am hungry!" he said.

Julian gave him what he had, an old piece of bacon and the crust of a black loaf. When he had devoured them, the table, the dish, and the handle of the knife bore the same spots that could be seen on his body.

Next he said, "I am thirsty!"

Julian went to get his pitcher, and it gave out an aroma, as he took it, which enlarged his heart and nostrils. It was wine—what happiness! But the Leper put out his arm and emptied the whole pitcher at a draught.

Then he said, "I am cold!"

And Julian, with his candle, set light to a pile of bracken in the middle of the hut.

The Leper came to warm himself, and as he crouched on his heels he trembled in every limb and weakened. His eyes ceased to gleam, his sores ran, and in an almost lifeless voice he murmured:

"Thy bed!"

Julian helped him gently to drag himself there, and even spread the canvas of his boat over him as a covering.

The Leper groaned. His teeth showed at the corners of his mouth, a faster rattle shook his chest, and as each breath was taken his body hollowed to the backbone.

Then he shut his eyes.

"It is like ice in my bones! Come close to me!"

And Julian, lifting the cloth, lay down on the dead leaves side by side with him.

The Leper turned his head.

"Take off thy clothes, that I may have thy body's warmth!"

Julian took off his clothes and lay down on the bed again, naked as when he was born; and he felt the Leper's skin against his thigh, colder than a serpent and rough as a file.

He tried to hearten him, and the other answered in gasps:

"Ah, I am dying!   Come closer, warm me! Not with the hands; no, with thy whole body!"

Julian stretched himself completely over him, mouth to mouth and chest on chest.

Then the Leper clasped him, and his eyes suddenly became as bright as stars; his hair drew out like sunbeams; the breath of his nostrils was as sweet as roses; a cloud of incense rose from the hearth, and the waves began to sing.   Meanwhile an abundance of delight, a superhuman joy flooded into Julian's soul as he lay swooning; and he who still clasped him in his arms grew taller, ever taller, until his head and feet touched the two walls of the hut.   The roof flew off, the firmament unrolled—and Julian rose towards the blue spaces, face to face with Our Lord Jesus, who carried him to heaven.

And that is the story of St. Julian the Hospitaller, more or less as you will find it on a church window in the region where I live.

HERODIAS

Herodias

I

THE citadel of Machærus rose east of the
Dead Sea on a basalt peak shaped like a cone,
girdled by four deep valleys; two about its
sides, one in front, and the fourth behind.
There were houses piled against its base inside a circling wall which rose and fell with the
uneven ground; and a zigzag road gashed in
the rock linked the town to the fortress, whose
ramparts were a hundred and twenty cubits
high with many angles, battlements along the
edge, and here and there towers, like diadems
in the stone crown hung over the abyss. Inside there was a palace ornamented with porticoes. It was roofed with a terrace which had
a balustrade of sycamore wood running round
it, and poles arranged for stretching an awning.

Before daybreak one morning the Tetrarch
Herod Antipas came out to lean on it and look
round him.

The mountains immediately under his eyes were beginning to unveil their crests, while their main bulk was still in shadow to the bottom of the chasms. A mist was floating; it parted, and the contours of the Dead Sea appeared. The dawn, rising behind Machærus, spread a glow of red. Soon it lit up the sands on the beach, the hills, the desert, and, still further, the mountains of Judea, and steepened their grey, knotted surfaces. Engedi drew its dark line across the middle, and Hebron rounded like a dome in the recess. Eshcol showed pomegranates, Sorek vines, and Karmel fields of sesame; and above Jerusalem rose the huge cube-like form of the tower of Antony. The Tetrarch looked away from it to contemplate the palm-trees of Jericho on the right. He thought of the other towns in his Galilee— Capernaum, Endor, Nazareth, and Tiberias —to which, perhaps, he would never return. And the Jordan flowed over the arid plain, absolutely white, and glistening like a snow-drift. The lake was now a sheet of lapis lazuli; and at its southern point, towards Yemen, Antipas recognized something he was afraid to see. There were brown tents sprinkled about; horses, and men with lances passing between them; and dying fires glittered like sparks on the ground. They were the troops of the king of the Arabs, whose daughter he had put away to take Herodias, the wife of one of his brothers who lived in Italy and made no claims to power.

Antipas was waiting for help from the Romans, gnawed with anxieties because Vitellius, the governor of Syria, was slow to appear.

Probably Agrippa had ruined his credit with the emperor. His third brother Philip, the ruler of Batanea, was arming secretly. The Jews were tired of his idolatrous ways, and everyone else was tired of his power; so much so that he was wavering between two schemes —either to conciliate the Arabs or make an alliance with the Parthians. On the pretext of celebrating his birthday he had invited the commanders of his troops, the stewards of his domains, and the chief men in Galilee to a great feast that very day.

He swept all the roads with a searching glance. They were empty. Eagles flew over his head, and the soldiers along the rampart were asleep against the walls. Nothing stirred inside the castle.

Suddenly a far-off voice, issuing seemingly out of the depths of the earth, made him turn pale. He bent down to listen; it had ceased.

It rose once more; he clapped his hands and called, "Mannæï! Mannæï!"

A man appeared, naked to the waist like the masseurs at baths. He was extremely tall, old, and lean, and wore a sword in a bronze sheath at his thigh. His hair was caught up with a comb, which made his forehead seem longer than it was. Sleepiness dulled the eyes; but his teeth glistened and his toes balanced lightly on the pavement. His whole body had the suppleness of a monkey, and his face was as impassive as a mummy's.

"Where is he?" asked the Tetrarch.

Mannæï pointed with his thumb to an object behind them, and replied, "Still there!"

"I thought I heard him!"

And Antipas drew a deep breath of relief and inquired about Iaokanan—the same whom the Latins call St. John the Baptist. He asked if anything more had been seen of the two men who were admitted to his cell as a favour a month or so before; had their object in coming been discovered?

Mannæï answered:

"They had some mysterious words with him, like thieves when they meet at a cross-roads in the evening. Then they went away towards upper Galilee, declaring that they would bring great tidings."

Antipas bent his head and then cried with an air of terror:

"Guard him! Guard him! And let no one enter! Close the door fast! Cover up the fosse! They must not even suspect he is alive!"

Mannæï had forestalled these orders on his own account; for Iaokanan was a Jew, and he hated the Jews, like all Samaritans. Their temple at Gerizim, which Moses had marked out for the centre of Israel, had vanished since the reign of Hyrcanus, and the Temple at Jerusalem roused them to fury as an outrage and a standing injustice. Mannæï had stolen into it to pollute the altar with dead men's bones. His companions were not so quick as he was and had been beheaded.

He saw it there, in the gap between two hills. The white marble walls and sheets of gold on its roofs shone brilliantly in the sun. It was like a translucent hill: a superhuman object that annihilated everything by its pride and splendour.

Then he stretched out his arms in the direction of Zion. With body erect, head thrown back, and fists clenched he hurled a curse at it, believing there was an efficacy in the words.

Antipas listened without appearing shocked.

The Samaritan spoke again: "He is restless at times, and would like to escape, hoping for deliverance. Other times he looks subdued, like a sick animal; or else I see him walking in the dark place, repeating, "What matters it? I must decrease that He may increase!"

Antipas and Mannaeï looked at each other; but the Tetrarch was weary of reflection. The mountains all round, like great waves petrified in layers, the dark chasms on the sides of the cliffs, the immense blue sky, the violent blaze of light, and the depth of the abysses troubled him. He was seized with depression at the look of the desert, and the suggestion of fallen amphitheatres and palaces in its crumbled surface. The hot wind brought a smell of sulphur like an exhalation from the accursed cities, buried under the banks of heavy waters. These signs of an eternal anger terrorized his thoughts; and he stayed there leaning his elbows on the balustrade, with his eyes fixed and his forehead in his hands. Someone touched him; he turned round. Herodias stood in front of him.

She was wrapped in a thin purple tunic down
to her sandals. She had left her chamber in
a hurry, without bracelets or ear-rings; a tress
of her black hair fell down over one arm, and
the end of it curled into the hollow of her
breasts. Her nostrils, which were excessively
arched, quivered; a joy of victory lit up her
face. She said in a loud voice which shook the
Tetrarch:

"Cæsar is our friend! Agrippa is in
prison!"

"Who has told thee?"

"I know it! It is because he wanted Caius
to be emperor," she added.

Agrippa, while living on their charity, had
intrigued for the title of king, which they
craved as eagerly as he did. There would be
no more fears in future. "Tiberius's dungeons
are hard to open, and life is not always safe
inside!"

Antipas took in her meaning, and though she
was Agrippa's sister he thought her abominable idea was justified. Such murders were
part of the logic of things—a fatality in royal
houses. In Herod's, people had stopped
counting them.

Then she gave the whole story of her venture—how Agrippa's clients had been bought,

his letters opened, spies posted at every door; and how she had managed to seduce Eutyches the informer.

"No cost was too high for me! And have I not done more than that, for thee? . . . I gave up my daughter!"

She had left the child in Rome after her divorce, confident that she would have others by the Tetrarch; but she never spoke of her, and he wondered what prompted this tender fit.

The awning had been spread and big cushions promptly brought to them. Herodias sank down there and began to cry, turning her back to him. Then she passed her hand over her eyes and said she did not want to think of it any more; she was happy as she was; and she reminded him of their talks there in the atrium, the meetings at the baths, their walks along the Sacred Way, and evenings in the great villas, by murmuring fountains, under arches of flowers, with the Roman Campagna before them. She looked at him as she used to look and brushed coaxingly against his chest. He pushed her away; the love she was trying to revive was so far off now! All his misfortunes flowed from it; war had been going on now for close upon twelve years. She had made the

Tetrarch older. The sombre, violet-edged toga betrayed his rounded shoulders. There were white hairs in his beard, and the sunshine came through the awning and lit up his troubled forehead. Herodias's brow was wrinkled too; and as they sat face to face they observed each other in strange fashion.

The mountain roads began to fill with people. Herdsmen pricked on oxen, children pulled at donkeys, grooms led horses along. Those who came down from the heights behind Machærus passed out of sight behind the castle; others climbed the ravine in front and unloaded their luggage in the courtyards when they reached the town. These were the Tetrarch's purveyors, and servants sent on in advance of his guests.

But to the left, at the end of the terrace, appeared an Essene, white-robed and barefooted; he had a stoical air. Mannæï made a rush at him from the right with his sword lifted.

"Slay him!" Herodias cried.

"Halt!" said the Tetrarch.

He stopped moving, and so did the other. They then retreated backwards by different staircases, without taking their eyes off each other.

"I know him," said Herodias; "his name is

Phanuel, and he is trying to see Iaokanan, as you are blind enough to keep the man alive."

Antipas urged that he might be of use some day. His attacks on Jerusalem brought the rest of the Jews over to their side.

"No!" she replied, "they will accept any master, and have not the strength to make a country of their own!" As for the man who stirred up the people with hopes cherished since Nehemiah's day, the best policy was to suppress him.

The Tetrarch thought there was no hurry. "Iaokanan dangerous! Why, come now!" He pretended to laugh at the idea.

"Be silent!" And again she told the story of how she had been humiliated when she went out towards Gilead one day to gather balsam. "There were people by the side of the river putting on their clothes. On a mound close by a man was speaking. He had a garment of camel's hair about his loins, and his head was like the head of a lion. As soon as he saw me he spat at me all the curses of the prophets. His eyes flamed, his voice roared; he raised his arms as though to pluck the thunder out of heaven. I could not flee—my chariot-wheels were in sand up to the axles. I drew away slowly, screened under my cloak, and those insults fell like storm-rain and froze me."

While Iaokanan lived she could not live. When he was seized and bound with cords the soldiers were to stab him if he resisted. He behaved submissively. Serpents had been put into his prison, and died there.

Herodias was exasperated by these futile ruses. Besides, why did he make war on her? The discourses which he cried aloud to crowds had spread abroad, and were circulating; she heard them everywhere, the air was full of them. Against armed legions she would have been brave enough, but this evasive force was more dangerous than swords, and paralysing. Pale with anger, she went to and fro on the terrace, lacking words to express what was stifling her.

She thought, besides, that the Tetrarch might yield to opinion and perhaps think of repudiating her. Then all would be lost! From her childhood onwards she had cherished the dream of a great empire. To win that she had left her first husband and turned to Antipas; and he, apparently, had duped her.

"A fine support I got by entering your family!"

"It is as good as yours," said the Tetrarch simply.

Herodias felt the ancestral blood of priests and kings boiling in her veins.

"Why, your grandfather was a sweeper in the temple of Ascalon! The rest were shepherds, robbers, caravan-drivers, a wretched horde tributary to Judah since King David! All my ancestors have vanquished yours! The first of the Maccabees drove you out of Hebron, Hyrcanus forced you to circumcize yourselves!" And breathing the patrician's contempt for the plebeian, the hatred of Jacob against Edom, she reproached him with his indifference to insults, his weakness towards the Pharisees who betrayed him, and his truckling to the people, who loathed him. "You are just like them—admit it! You are pining for the Arab girl who dances round her stones! Take her back, then! Go and live with her under her canvas roof; devour the bread she has baked under the ashes; swallow the curdled milk from her sheep—kiss her blue cheeks—and forget me!"

The Tetrarch had ceased to listen. He was looking at a house with a flat roof, on which he saw a girl and an old woman who held a

parasol with a reed handle as long as a fisher-
man's rod. A big travelling basket lay open
in the middle of the carpet; girdles, veils, gold
and silver pendants flowed over in confusion.
The girl bent towards these things at intervals
and shook them in the air. She was dressed
like a Roman girl in a curly tunic and a peplum
with emerald tassels; blue bands kept back her
hair, which no doubt was too heavy for her,
as she lifted her hand to it from time to time.
She was half hidden by the moving shadow
of the parasol above. Two or three times
Antipas caught sight of her delicate neck, the
turn of an eye, the corner of a little mouth.
But he could see the whole of her figure, from
the hips to the neck, bending and then drawing
lissomely up again. He watched for the return of that movement, and his breathing became louder; a flame lit in his eyes. Herodias
observed him.

"Who is it?" he asked.

She replied that she had no idea, and went
away suddenly quieted.

Under the porticoes were some Galileans
waiting for the Tetrarch—the chief scribe, the
superintendent of the pastures, the manager of
the salt-pits, and a Babylonian Jew who com-

manded his horsemen. All saluted him with
one voice, and he disappeared towards the in-
ner rooms.

At the angle of a corridor Phanuel sprang up.

"Ah, thou again! Art come to see Iaokanan, no doubt?"

"And thee also! I have a weighty thing
to tell thee." He kept near Antipas, and
followed him into a dim room. The light
fell through a grating which opened all along
under the cornice. The walls were painted a
deep red colour, almost black. At the end
of the room spread an ebony bed, with ox-hide
straps; and a golden shield above it gleamed
like a sun.

Antipas paced the length of the big room
and lay down on the bed. Phanuel remained
standing. He lifted his arm and said with an
inspired air:

"The Most High sends a son of His from
time to time. Iaokanan is one. Use him
cruelly and thou wilt be punished."

"It is he who persecutes me!" cried Antipas.
"He asked me for an act which I could not
perform, and since that time he has rent me
to pieces. I was not harsh to begin with! He
has even sent men out from Machærus who
are turning my province upside down. Woe to

his life! As he attacks me, I must defend myself!"

"His fits of rage are over-violent," Phanuel answered. "But no matter; he must be set free."

"One does not set savage beasts free," said the Tetrarch.

"Have no more anxiety," the Essene replied. "He will go to the Arabs, Gauls, and Scythians. His work has to spread to the ends of the earth!"

Antipas seemed lost in a vision. "His power is mighty. . . . I love him in spite of myself!"

"You will free him, then?"

The Tetrarch shook his head. He was afraid of Herodias, Mannæï—and the unknown.

Phanuel tried to persuade him, declaring as a guarantee of his plans that the Essenes would submit to the kings. People respected these poor men, dressed in flax, who were inflexible under torture and read the future in the stars.

Antipas remembered something that had fallen from Phanuel just before.

"What is this matter which as thou saidst was important?"

A negro appeared. His body was white

with dust; his voice rattled, and he could only say:

"Vitellius!"

"What? He is coming?"

"I have seen him. Less than three hours, and he is here!"

The curtains in the corridors tossed as if the wind shook them. The castle became alive with noise—a din of people hurrying, furniture being dragged about, and plate falling; and trumpets sounded from the tops of the towers to warn the scattered slaves.

II

The ramparts swarmed with people when Vitellius entered the courtyard, leaning on his interpreter's arm. A large red litter decked with plumes and mirrors came behind. He was wearing the toga, laticlave, and laced boots of a consul, and had a group of lictors round him.

Their twelve bundles of rods, with a hatchet in the middle and fastened by a thong, were planted against the gate; and then the crowd trembled before the majesty of the Roman people.

The litter, handled by eight men, came to a

stop.   There emerged from it a youth with a large stomach, a blotched face, and a row of pearls along his fingers.   They offered him a cup full of wine and spiced herbs; he drank it, and asked for another.

The Tetrarch had fallen at the pro-consul's knees, saying how distressed he was not to have heard before of the favour of his presence. Otherwise he would have ordered the honours due to the Vitellii to be paid them all along their route, for they were descended from the goddess Vitellia, and a road from the Janiculum to the sea still bore their name. There had been quæstorships and consulships past counting in their family; and Lucius, who was now his guest, deserved special thanks as the conqueror of the Clites and father of the youthful Aulus, who might be said to be returning to his own domain, for the East was the home of the gods.   These extravagances were uttered in Latin and Vitellius received them impassively.

He replied that Herod the Great was enough to make a nation's glory.   The Athenians had made him supervisor of the Olympic games; he had built temples in honour of Augustus, and been patient, resourceful, redoubtable, and always loyal to the Cæsars.

Then between the columns with bronze capitals Herodias was seen advancing with the air of an empress, surrounded by women and eunuchs carrying lighted perfumes on silver-gilt dishes. The proconsul took three steps to meet her, and she saluted him with an inclination of her head, and cried:

"What happiness that Agrippa, the enemy of Tiberius, should henceforward be powerless to do harm!"

Vitellius did not know of that event and thought her dangerous; and when Antipas swore that he would do anything for the emperor, he put in:

"Even if other people suffered by it?"

He had secured hostages from the king of the Parthians, but the emperor no longer thought of that; because Antipas, who was at the conference and wanted to make an impression, had sent news of the matter at once. Thence came a deep hatred on Vitellius's part, and his delay in assisting Herod.

The Tetrarch stuttered; but Aulus said with a laugh:

"Be calm! I will protect you!"

The proconsul pretended not to have heard. The father's prospects hung on the defilement of his son; and this flower out of the mud of

Capreæ procured Vitellius such immense advantages that every attention was paid him, though, as a poisonous flower, he was distrusted.

A tumult rose below the gate. A file of white mules was led in, ridden by personages wearing the dress of priests. They were Sadducees and Pharisees, drawn to Machærus by the same ambition: the first wanted to capture the high-priesthood and the latter to keep it. Their faces were grim, especially those of the Pharisees, who were hostile to Rome and the Tetrarch. The skirts of their tunics embarrassed them in the turmoil, and the tiaras wobbled on their foreheads above the slips of written parchment.

Almost at the same moment came in soldiers belonging to the advance-guard. Their shields had been cased in sacks, as a precaution against the dust; and behind them was Marcellus, the proconsul's lieutenant, with publicans who gripped wooden tablets under their arms.

Antipas presented the chief men about him —Tolmaï, Kanthera, Sehon, Ammonius of Alexandria, who bought asphalte for him, Naaman, the captain of his light infantry, and Iaçim the Babylonian.

Vitellius had noticed Mannæï. "That fel-

low there, what is he?" A gesture of the Tetrarch's conveyed that he was the executioner.

Then he introduced the Sadducees. Jonathas, a little person with a free manner who
spoke Greek, besought the master to honour
them with a visit at Jerusalem. He replied
that probably he would.

Eleazar, with a hooked nose and a long
beard, asked on behalf of the Pharisees for the
high priest's cloak which was detained in the
tower of Antony by the civil authority. After that the Galileans denounced Pontius Pi-
late: on an occasion when a lunatic was hunting
for David's golden vases in a cave near Sa-
maria he had killed some of the inhabitants.
They all spoke at once, Mannæï more violently
than any. Vitellius declared that the guilty
would be punished.

Cries broke out in front of a portico, where
the soldiers had hung up their shields. Now
the coverings had been taken off, Cæsar's
effigy was visible on the bosses. This, to the
Jews, was idolatry. Antipas harangued them,
while Vitellius, who was on a raised seat in the
colonnade, grew astonished at their fury. Tiberius had certainly been right to banish four
hundred of them to Sardinia. But in their

own country they were strong—and he gave
orders to take down the shields.

Then the proconsul was surrounded with
them, begging for the redress of wrongs, for
privileges and charity. Their clothes were
torn, they crushed each other, and slaves hit
right and left with sticks to make room. The
people nearest the gate began to go down the
lane, and then, as others came up it, flowed
back; and there was a cross-current in the surg-
ing mass penned by the enclosure of the walls.

Vitellius asked why there were so many people. Antipas explained that his birthday feast
was the cause, and pointed to some of his
household who were leaning over the battlements and pulling up huge basketfuls of meat,
fruit, and vegetables, whole antelopes and
storks, large azure-coloured fish, and grapes,
melons, and pomegranates heaped up in pyra-
mids. It was more than Aulus could bear.
He made a dash for the kitchens, carried away
by that historic greed which was to astonish
the world.

As he passed a cellar he noticed some dishes
that were like breast-plates. Vitellius came
and looked at them, and insisted on being
shown the underground rooms in the fortress.

They were cut in high vaults out of the rock, with pillars at regular distances. The first contained old armour, but the second was packed with spears, all their points projecting out of tufts of feathers. The third looked as if it were carpeted with reed mats, the slim arrows lay so straight and close together. Scimitar blades covered the walls of the fourth room. In the middle of the fifth were rows of helmets, whose crests looked like a regiment of red snakes. In the sixth nothing was to be seen but quivers; in the seventh, greaves; in the eighth, arm-plates; while in the others were forks, grappling-irons, ladders, ropes—even poles for the catapults and bells for the chests of the dromedaries! And as the hill widened to its base, hollowed out inside like a bee-hive, there were still deeper and more numerous chambers under these.

Vitellius, with his interpreter Phineas, and Sisenna the chief publican, went round them by the light of torches borne by three eunuchs. In the gloom they made out hideous objects which the barbarians had invented: maces studded with nails, poisoned javelins, pincers like a crocodile's jaws. In short, the Tetrarch owned material of war at Machærus for forty thousand men.

He had collected it in view of his enemies
allying. But the proconsul might think, or
say, that it was to fight the Romans, and he
cast about for explanations. What should he
say? That they were not his; that many of
them were used in self-defence against brig-
ands; that some, too, were needed against the
Arabs; or else that the whole array had been
his father's? And instead of walking behind
the proconsul he went in front with rapid
strides. Then he placed himself against
the wall, extending his elbows so as to screen
it with his toga; but there, above his head, was
the top of a door. Vitellius observed it, and
wanted to know what was inside.

The Babylonian alone could open it.

"Call the Babylonian!"

They waited for him. His father had come
from the banks of the Euphrates to offer himself and five hundred horse to Herod the Great
for the defence of the eastern frontiers. When
the kingdom was divided Iaçim had stayed
with Philip, and was now in the service of
Antipas.

He appeared, with a bow at his shoulder and
a whip in his hand. His crooked legs were
wound tightly with many-coloured garters.
His big arms emerged out of a sleeveless tunic,

and a fur bonnet shaded his face; the beard
was curled in ringlets.

He seemed, at first, not to understand the
interpreter. But Vitellius threw a look at
Antipas, who promptly repeated his order.
Then Iaçim placed both his hands against the
door and it slid into the wall.

Out of the darkness came a breath of warm
air. A winding passage led downwards; they
took it, and reached the threshold of a cavern,
more extensive than the other vaults. The
end of it opened into an arcade above the precipice which defended the citadel on that side.
A honeysuckle plant clung to the roof, letting
its flowers hang down full in the light. Over
the surface of the floor murmured a trickle of
water.

White horses were there, a hundred perhaps,
eating barley from a shelf on a level with their
mouths. They had their manes painted blue,
their hoofs in mittens of esparto grass, and
the hair between their ears puffed over their
foreheads like a wig. They whisked their
flowing tails gently against their legs. The
proconsul was struck dumb with admiration.

Marvellous animals they were, supple as
snakes and light as birds. They would be off
when the rider shot his arrow, overthrow men

with a bite in the stomach, extricate themselves
from hard places in the rocks, jump chasms,
and keep up a frenzied gallop on the plains
for a whole day; a word would stop them. As
soon as Iaçim went in they came to him like
sheep at the sight of a shepherd, and stretching
out their necks looked at him with child-like,
questioning eyes. From force of habit he uttered a deep, hoarse cry which roused their
spirits, and they reared up hungry for the open,
begging to run free.

Antipas had shut them up in this place, which
was kept for the animals in case of a siege,
for fear that Vitellius might carry them
off.

"It is a bad stable," said the proconsul,
"and you run a risk of losing them. Make an
inventory, Sisenna!"

The publican drew a tablet out of his girdle,
counted the horses, and wrote them down.
The agents of the tax companies corrupted the
governors in order to pillage the provinces.
This fellow, with his weasel's jaw and blink-
ing eyes, sniffed about everywhere.

Finally they went up to the courtyard again.
There were round brass plates here and
there in the middle of the flagstones, covering
the cisterns. Vitellius noticed one which was

larger than the others, and did not ring underfoot as they did. He struck them all in turn, and then shouted, stamping:

"I have it! I have it! Herod's treasure is here!"

The quest for his treasures was a passion with the Romans. The Tetrarch swore that they did not exist. What was underneath, then?

"Oh, nothing! A man—a prisoner."

"Show me him!" said Vitellius.

The Tetrarch did not obey; the Jews would have found out his secret. His reluctance to lift the cover made Vitellius impatient.

"Break it in!" he cried to the lictors.

Mannæï had guessed what was interesting them. The sight of an axe made him think that Iaokanan was going to be beheaded; and stopping the lictor at the first blow on the plate he inserted a sort of hook between it and the pavement and then stiffened his long, thin arms and raised it gently. It fell back, everyone admiring the old man's strength. The cover, which was lined with wood, disclosed a trap-door of the same size; at a blow from the fist it folded into two panels. Then the mouth of a huge pit came into view, with an unrailed staircase winding round it, and those who

leaned over the edge saw something dimly
alarming at the bottom.

A human being lay on the ground, covered
with long hair which seemed one with the hairy
garment on his back. He got up. His forehead touched a grating, fixed horizontally
across the pit; and from time to time he vanished into the depths of his cave.

The sunshine glittered on the crests of the
diadems, on the sword-hilts, and made the
pavement desperately hot; doves flew out of
the cornices and wheeled above the courtyard.
It was the time when Mannæï usually threw
grain to them. He was now crouching in
front of the Tetrarch, who stood near Vitellius. The Galileans, priests, and soldiers
formed a ring behind; and all, strained with
apprehension of what would happen next, were
silent.

First, in a sepulchral voice, came a loud sigh.

Herodias heard it at the other end of the
palace. Yielding to a fascination, she passed
through the crowd and bent forward to listen,
with one hand on Mannæï's shoulder.

The voice rose:

"Woe unto you, Pharisees and Sadducees, ye
offspring of vipers, swollen wineskins, tinkling
cymbals!"

It was Iaokanan, they knew. His name went round, and more listeners hastened up.

"Woe unto thee, O people! Woe to the traitors of Judah and the drunkards of Ephraim, to those who dwell in the fat valley and stagger with fumes of wine!

"Let them pass away as water that floweth, as the slug which melteth in its going, as the dead child in the womb that doth not see the sun.

"Then must thou, Moab, flee into the cypresses like the sparrows, and like jerboas into the caves. The gates of the fortresses shall be broken faster than nut-shells, the walls shall crumble, the towns shall burn; and the flail of the Everlasting shall not halt. It shall turn your limbs over in your own blood, like wool in a dyer's vat; it shall tear you like a new harrow; it shall scatter all the morsels of your flesh upon the hills!"

Of what conqueror was he speaking? Was it Vitellius? None but the Romans could exterminate like that. Murmurs began to escape from the crowd—"Enough, enough! Let him cease!"

He went on, still louder:

"The little children shall crawl on ashes by

the corpses of their mothers. A man shall go by night to seek his bread among the ruins, in peril of the sword. The jackals shall snatch bones from one another in the public places, where the old men conversed at evening. Thy virgins, swallowing their tears, shall play the lute at the stranger's banquets, and the backs of thy most valiant sons shall stoop and be flayed with burdens that are too heavy!"

The days of their exile passed before the people's eyes, and all the calamities of their history. These were the words of the prophets of old. Iaokanan flung them out like mighty blows, one after another.

But the voice softened now to a rhythmical chant. He proclaimed a dawn of freedom and glorious signs in the sky. The new-born child should put his arm into a dragon's den; there should be gold where clay was, and the wilderness would blossom like a rose. "That which is sold now for sixty kissars shall not cost a farthing. From the rocks shall gush springs of milk; men shall fall asleep in the wine-presses with a full belly. When comest thou, O thou whom I hope for? Against thy coming shall all the people kneel, and thy dominion shall be everlasting, O Son of David!"

The Tetrarch flung himself back; the existence of a Son of David was an insult to him, and a threat.

Iaokanan attacked him for his kingship: "There is no king save the Everlasting!"— and for his gardens, statues, and ivory furniture, like the ungodly Ahab's.

Antipas broke the little cord on which the seal hung at his breast, and threw the seal into the pit with an order to the prophet to be silent.

The voice replied:

"I will howl like a bear, like a wild ass, like a woman in her travail! Thine incest is chastised already, for God visits thee with the barrenness of a mule!"

And laughs came up, with a noise like splashing waves.

Vitellius persisted in staying there. The interpreter, with an unmoved voice, repeated in the language of the Romans all the insults which Iaokanan bellowed in his own, so that the Tetrarch and Herodias were compelled to submit to them twice over. He was panting, and she stared open-mouthed at the bottom of the pit.

The dreadful man turned his head up, and

clutching the bars glued a face to them like a
tangle of briars with two gleaming coals:

"Ah! it is thou, Jezabel.

"Thou hast taken his heart with the creaking
of thy slipper; though neighedst like a mare.
Thou hast set up thy bed upon the mountains,
for the performance of thy sacrifices!

"The Lord shall tear off thine ear-rings, thy
purple robes, thy linen veils, the bracelets on
thine arms, the rings upon thy feet, and the
little crescents of gold that quiver on thy forehead; thy silver mirrors, thy fans of ostrich
feathers, the soles of pearl which make thee
tall, the pride of thy diamonds, the perfumes
of thy hair, the painting on thy nails, all the
devices of thy luxury; and there shall not
be pebbles enough to stone the adulterous
woman!"

She looked round in search of a defender.
The Pharisees hypocritically lowered their
eyes; the Sadducees turned their heads away
in fear of offending the proconsul. Antipas
looked as if he were expiring.

Louder and deeper, now, the voice rumbled
and broke like claps of thunder; and as the
mountain echo took it up it swept Machærus
with reiterated crashes.

"Stretch thyself in the dust, daughter of Babylon, grind thy flour, take off thy girdle, unloose thy shoe, truss up thy garments, cross the rivers! Thy shame shall be discovered; thine abomination shall be seen. Thy teeth shall be broken with the force of thy sobbing. The Everlasting loathes the stench of thy misdoings! Accursed, accursed one, die like a dog!"

The trap was shut and the cover fell back on it. Mannæï was longing to strangle Iaokanan.

Herodias disappeared. Antipas proceeded to justify himself among the scandalized Pharisees.

"Doubtless a man must marry his brother's wife," replied Eleazar, "but Herodias was not a widow, and besides she had a child, which makes the abomination in the case."

"Wrong, wrong!" contended Jonathas the Sadducee. "The Law condemns these marriages, but does not proscribe them utterly."

"No matter, people are highly unjust to me," said Antipas, "for Absalom, in point of fact, lay with his father's wives, Judah with his daughter-in-law, Ammon with his sister, Lot with his daughters."

Aulus, who had been asleep, reappeared at

that moment. When the question was explained to him he took the side of the Tetrarch. It was absurd to let nonsense like that stand in one's way; and Aulus was much amused by the censure of the priests and Iaokanan's fury.

Herodias turned round towards him from the middle of the palace steps:

"Thou art wrong, my lord! He is telling the people to refuse to pay taxes."

"Is that true?" asked the publican promptly.

The replies were affirmative in the main, and the Tetrarch confirmed them.

Vitellius thought that the prisoner might escape; and as the behaviour of Antipas seemed doubtful he posted sentinels at the gates, along the walls, and in the courtyard. Then he went off towards his rooms, accompanied by the priestly deputations. Each party uttered their complaints, though they kept off the question of the high-priestship. Finding himself besieged by them all, he dismissed them.

As Jonathas was taking leave he saw Antipas, in an embrasure, talking to a long-haired man dressed in white—an Essene—and he felt sorry that he had supported him.

There was one reflection which comforted the Tetrarch: Iaokanan was his concern no longer, for the Romans were taking him over. It was a great relief.

Phanuel was walking on the path round the walls at the moment. He called him and said, pointing to the soldiers:—

"They are the stronger! It is no fault of mine—I cannot set him free!"

The courtyard was empty; the slaves were resting. The red sky set the horizon in a flame, and the smallest upright objects stood out black against it. Antipas made out the salt works at the farther end of the Dead Sea, but the tents of the Arabs were no longer visible. They had gone off, probably. The moon was rising, and a feeling of peace descended on him.

Phanuel remained with his chin sunk on his breast, in utter dejection. At last he brought out what he had to say. Ever since the beginning of the month he had been studying the heavens before dawn, where the constellation of Perseus was then at the zenith. Agala was barely manifest, Algol was less brilliant, and Mira Coeti had disappeared. From all this he augured the death of a man of importance, that very night, in Machærus.

Who could it be? Vitellius was too well guarded. They would not execute Iaokanan.

"It must be I, then," mused the Tetrarch. Perhaps the Arabs meant to come back—or the proconsul might discover his overtures to the Parthians! And there were cut-throats from Jerusalem escorting the priests, with daggers under their clothes; the Tetrarch had no doubts of Phanuel's science.

He thought of turning to Herodias. He hated her, no doubt, but she would give him courage;. and the links of the enchantment which once bound him were not quite broken.

He entered her room. Cinnamon was smoking on a porphyry basin; powders, unguents, stuffs airy as clouds, embroideries lighter than feathers, were scattered about.

He said nothing of Phanuel's prediction, nor of his fear of Jews and Arabs; she would only have called him a coward. He merely spoke of the Romans. Vitellius had not breathed a word of his military plans; and Antipas imagining him to be a friend of Caius, who was courted by Agrippa, saw himself being exiled or perhaps having his throat cut.

Herodias humoured him contemptuously, tried to reassure him, and finally took out of a little box an odd-looking medal, stamped with the head of Tiberius. "That will make the lictors turn pale and accusations melt

away." The Tetrarch was stirred to gratitude, and asked how she came to have it. "It
was given to me," she replied.

A bare arm emerged under a curtain in front
of them; it was a delicious young arm which
might have been modelled in ivory by Poly-
cletus. There was a grace in its slight awk-
wardness as it wavered in the air to pick up
a tunic left behind on a stool near the wall.
An old woman pulled back the curtain and
passed this gently in.

A vague recollection came into the Tetrarch's mind.

"Does that slave belong to thee?" he asked
Herodias.

"What concern is it of thine?" she answered.

III

The banqueting hall was thronged with
guests. It had three aisles, like a basilica,
divided by pillars of almug wood with bronze
capitals carved all over. They supported
two galleries with open work in front; and a
third in golden filigree curved out from the
back of the hall, facing an enormous arch at
the other end.

Candelabra burned on the tables which lined

the whole interior, making fiery sheaves among
the cups of painted earthenware and the cop-
per dishes, the cubes of snow and piles of
grapes; but under that lofty vaulting their red
glow lessened steadily, and points of light
shone as stars do through the branches of trees
at night. Through the opening of the great
bay torches could be seen on the flat tops of
the houses; Antipas was feasting his friends,
his people, and all who chose to come.

Slaves, alert as dogs, moved to and fro carrying dishes, with felt slippers over their toes.

The proconsul's table took up a dais par-
queted with sycamore, underneath the gilded
tribune. This was enclosed like a kind of
pavilion by tapestries from Babylon. Three
ivory couches, one facing the hall and two at
the sides, held Vitellius, his son, and Antipas;
the proconsul was on the left near the door,
Aulus on the right, and the Tetrarch in the
middle.

He wore a heavy black cloak whose material was hardly visible below the colours laid
on it, the rouge on his cheek-bones, the fan-
shaped beard, and blue-powdered hair clasped
by a diadem of jewels. Vitellius kept on his
purple shoulder-belt, which slanted downwards
across a linen toga. Aulus, who wore a violet

silk robe with silver plaques, had had its
sleeves tied back behind him.   His hair was in
ringlets, curled in layers, and a sapphire neck-
lace sparkled on his bosom, full and white as
a woman's.   On a mat close by him a beautiful
child sat cross-legged, and always smiling.
Aulus had seen him in the kitchens, and could
not part with him; finding it hard to remember
his Syrian name, he called him simply "the
Asiatic."   From time to time he stretched himself on his couch, and then his bare feet domi-
nated the company.

On his side sat the priests and officers of
Antipas, some residents from Jerusalem, and
the chief men of the Greek towns.   Below the
proconsul were Marcellus and the publican,
some of the Tetrarch's friends, and the nota-
bles of Cana, Ptolemais, and Jericho; then,
pell-mell, came mountaineers from the Lebanon
and old soldiers of Herod; twelve Thracians,
a Gaul, two Germans, gazelle hunters, Edo-
mite shepherds, the Sultan of Palmyra, sailors
from Ezion-geber.   Each had a cake of soft
paste before him to wipe his fingers on; and
with their arms, which craned like vulture's
necks, they took olives, pistachio nuts, and
almonds.   All had gay faces under their coro-
nals of flowers.

The Pharisees had spurned these as an indecency from Rome. They shuddered when they were sprinkled with galbanum and incense, a mixture reserved for use in the Temple. Aulus rubbed his arm-pits with this, and Antipas promised him a whole consignment of it, and three coffers of the true balm which had made Cleopatra greedy for Palestine.

A captain just arrived from his garrison at Tiberias had placed himself behind Antipas to tell him of some extraordinary occurrences; but the Tetrarch's attention was divided between the proconsul and what was being said at the neighbouring tables. They were talking of Iaokanan and other people of the kind. Simon of Gitti cleansed sins with fire; a certain Jesus . . .

"The worst of them all," cried Eleazar. "A wretched mountebank!"

A man rose behind the Tetrarch, pale as the hem of his chlamys. He came down from the dais and interrupted the Pharisees:

"That is a lie! Jesus works miracles!"

Antipas wanted to see some. "You ought to have brought him with you! Tell us about them."

And then he told how he, Jacob, having a sick daughter, had betaken himself to Caper-

naum to entreat the Master's will to heal her.
"Return to thy home; she is healed," the Master replied. And he had found her at the door, she having left her bed when the palace dial marked the third hour, which was the very moment when he approached Jesus.

Certainly, argued the Pharisees, potent herbs and practices existed. Here even, at Machærus, you sometimes found the baras which makes men invulnerable. But to heal without seeing or touching the sick person was impossible, unless Jesus made use of demons.

And the friends of Antipas, the chief men of Galilee, answered with a shake of the head: "Demons, evidently."

Jacob, standing between their table and the table of the priests, remained gently but proudly silent.

They called on him to speak: "Justify his power!"

He bowed his shoulders and said in a low voice, slowly, as if he were afraid of his own words:

"You know not, then, that He is the Messiah?"

All the priests looked at one another; and Vitellius asked what the word meant.

His interpreter waited a minute before answering. It was their name for a liberator who would bring them the enjoyment of all the goods of the earth and the dominion over all peoples. Some even held that two were to be expected. The first would be vanquished by Gog and Magog, demons of the north, but the other would exterminate the Prince of Evil; and for centuries they had waited for him to appear at any minute.

The priests having consulted each other, Eleazar began to speak. To begin with, he said, the Messiah would be David's son, and not a carpenter's. He would confirm the law; this Nazarene assailed it. And there was a yet stronger argument: He should have been heralded by the coming of Elias.

"But Elias *is* come!" Jacob retorted.

"Elias! Elias!" repeated the crowd, down to the extreme end of the hall. All saw, in their imagination, an old man with ravens flying overhead, an altar set on fire by lightning, and idolatrous priests being thrown into the streams; the women in the tribunes thought of the widow of Sarepta.

Jacob repeated until he was tired that he knew him. He had seen him, and the people had seen him as well!

"His name?"

Then he cried with all his strength, "Iaokanan!"

Antipas fell back as if he had been struck full in the chest. The Sadducees made a rush for Jacob. Eleazar went on declaiming till he could get a hearing. When silence was established he gathered his cloak round him and put questions like a judge.

"Inasmuch as the prophet is dead . . ."

Murmurs interrupted him. It was believed that Elias had only disappeared. He broke out angrily against the crowd, and then resumed his inquiry.

"Thou thinkest that he has come to life again?"

"Why not?" said Jacob.

The Sadducees shrugged their shoulders; Jonathas opened his little eyes wide and forced out a cackle of laughter. What could be sillier than the body's claim to everlasting life? For the proconsul's edification he recited a contemporary poet's line:

"Once dead it grows not, seems not to endure."

Just then Aulus leant over the edge of his couch with a perspiring brow; his face was green, his hands clenched on his stomach.

The Sadducees feigned great emotion and got the high-priesthood back next day as a reward. Antipas made a show of despair; Vitellius remained immovable. His anxiety, all the same, was poignant; for with his son went his fortune.

But Aulus had not finished the process of vomiting before he was anxious to eat again.

"Give me some marble dust, schist of Naxos, sea-water, anything! Supposing I took a bath?"

He chewed some snow, and then, after wavering between a pâté of Commagene and pink blackbirds, decided for pumpkins served with honey. The Asiatic gazed at him; such a capacity for absorbing food marked him as a portentous and superior being.

They served ox-kidneys, dormice, nightingales, minced meat in vine-leaves; and the priests discussed the problem of resurrection. Ammonius, a pupil of Philo the Platonist, considered them stupid, and said as much to some Greeks who were making fun of oracles. Marcellus and Jacob had struck up an alliance. The first was telling the second of the happiness he had experienced on being baptised into Mithras, and Jacob was pressing him to follow Jesus. Palm and tamarisk wine, wines of Safet and Byblus flowed from pitchers into bowls, from bowls into cups, from cups to throats; men chattered and their hearts grew expansive. Iaçim, a Jew, did not conceal his adoration of the stars. A merchant from Aphaka astounded the nomads by describing the wonders of the temple at Hierapolis; they asked how much the pilgrimage would cost. Others clung fast to the religion of their birth. A German who was nearly blind sang a hymn to celebrate the Scandinavian promontory where the gods appear with halos round their faces; and there were folk from Shechem who would not eat turtle-doves, out of respect for the dove Azima.

Groups stood talking in the middle of the hall; the steam of human breath joined the smoke from the candelabra and made a fog in the air. Phanuel passed along the wall. He had just been studying the firmament again, but as he was afraid of smears of oil—a great pollution for the Essenes—he did not go up to join the Tetrarch.

There was a noise of blows upon the castle gate. It was now known that Iaokanan was in custody there. Men were climbing up the path with torches; there was a dark, seething mass in the ravine, and from time to time they yelled, "Iaokanan! Iaokanan!"

"He is upsetting everything!" said Jonathas.

"There will be no more money if he goes on," the Pharisees added.

There was a dropping fire of recriminations. "Protect us!" "Make an end of him!" "Thou art deserting religion!" "Ungodly like all the Herods!"

"Less so than you!" retorted Antipas. "My father built your temple!"

Then the Pharisees, the sons of the proscribed and the partizans of Matathias, taxed him with the crimes of his family. Some had tapering skulls, stubbly beards, and weak, unpleasant hands; and others snub-nosed faces, with big round eyes and a bull-dog air. One group of a dozen, scribes and attendants on the priests, who fed themselves on the leavings of the sacrifice, made a rush as far as the bottom of the dais and threatened Antipas with knives. He harangued them, with a tepid support from the Sadducees. Catching sight of Mannæï he made signs to him to go away, as Vitellius implied by a look that this was no affair for him.

The Pharisees, who remained on their couches, worked themselves into a demoniacal rage and smashed the plates in front of them. They had been served with a stew of wild ass, the favourite dish of Mæcenas, which was an unclean food. Aulus mocked them about the ass's head, which they were said to revere, and fired off some more sarcasms on their aversion to the hog. Probably it was because that stout beast had slain their Bacchus. They were really too fond of wine; had not a golden vine been found in the temple?

The priests did not understand what he was saying. Phineas, a Galilean by origin, refused to translate it. This made him excessively angry, all the more as the Asiatic had disappeared in terror and the banquet was not to his taste. The food was vulgar and insufficiently dressed. He grew calm on seeing a dish of Syrian sheep-tails—perfect rolls of fat.

To Vitellius the character of the Jews seemed hideous. Their God might well be Moloch, whose altars he had encountered on the road. He remembered the sacrifices of children, and the story of the man who was mysteriously fattened up. He turned sick with disgust, like the Latin he was, at their intolerance, their frenzy against images, their brutal obstinacy. In fact, he wanted to leave, but Aulus refused. He had pushed his robe down to his thighs and now lay behind a pile of eatables, too gorged to take any, but determined not to leave them.

The people's exalted mood grew higher, and they gave themselves up to dreams of independence. They recalled the glories of Israel and how every conqueror had been punished— Antigonus, Crassus, Varus. . . .

"Curs!" said the proconsul—for he understood Syriac, and the only function of his interpreter was to give him more time to answer. Antipas swiftly drew out the emperor's medal, and looking tremblingly at Vitellius presented it with the effigy upmost.

Suddenly the panels of the golden tribune folded back, and in a sheen of tapers, amidst slaves and garlands of anemones, Herodias appeared. She was capped with an Assyrian mitre, attached to her forehead by a band which went under her chin; her hair flowed in ringlets over a scarlet peplum, slit down the length of the sleeves. As she stood between the two stone monsters, similar to those in the treasure of the Atreids, which rose by the door, she looked like a Cybele with her lions at her side. With a bowl in her hands she called from the high balustrade above Antipas:

"Long life to Cæsar!"

Vitellius, Antipas, and the priests echoed her homage.

But from the bottom of the hall came a hum of admiring surprise. A young girl had just entered.

Although her head and breast were hidden in a bluish veil the arch of her eyes, her ears like milky agates, and the whiteness of her skin could be seen through it. A square of shot silk covered her shoulders, and was fastened to her loins with a jewelled girdle. Her black drawers were sprigged with mandrakes, and she lazily clattered a pair of little shoes made from the down of humming-birds.

Having mounted the dais, she drew aside her veil. It was Herodias, just as she used to be in youth. Then she began to dance.

Her feet hovered in front of each other to the measure of the flute and a pair of castanets. Her rounded arms seemed to call someone who was for ever fleeing. Lighter than a butter-fly she chased him, like an inquiring Psyche, a roaming spirit, and seemed as though in a moment she would fly away.

The castanets gave place to a sound of melancholy little flutes. It was dejection following on hope. Her poses were the embodiment of sighs, and there was such a languor in all her being that one could not tell whether she were weeping for a god or swooning in his arms.

The eyes were half-shut, and her body writhed; she swayed her stomach like an undulating wave, made her breasts quiver. And yet her face remained motionless and her feet never stopped.

Vitellius compared her to Mnester, the mime; Aulus was still vomiting; the Tetrarch was lost in a dream and had ceased to think about Herodias. He fancied he saw her near the Sadducees. The apparition moved away.

But it was no apparition. It was Salome, the daughter of Herodias, whom her mother had had trained far away from Machærus to capture the Tetrarch's heart. The idea was a good one; she felt sure of it now.

The girl mimed the passionate desire which insists on being slaked. She danced like the Indian priestesses, the Nubians of the cataracts, the Mænads of Lydia. She bent over from side to side like a flower tossed in a storm. The brilliants leaped in her ears, the vest on her back flashed iridescently; and invisible sparks shot from her arms, feet, and clothes which set men on fire. A harp sounded, and the crowd applauded in answer. Salome opened her legs and, keeping her knees rigid, bent so low that her chin touched the floor; and the desert-dwellers schooled in abstinence, the Roman soldiers expert in debauchery, the greedy publicans and old priests embittered by disputes all panted greedily, with their nostrils dilated.

Then she circled frenziedly, as if in a mad round of witches, about Herod's table; and he said to her "Come! come!" in a voice broken by sobs of passion. She went on turning; the timbrels crashed as if they would burst, and the crowd yelled. But the Tetrarch cried still louder: "Come, come to me! Thou shalt have Capernaum! The plain of Tiberias— my citadels—the half of my kingdom!"

She threw herself on to her hands, with her heels in the air, scoured the dais thus like a large beetle, and then stopped abruptly. Her neck and spine were at right angles; the sheaths of colour round her legs went on like rainbows over her shoulders and framed her face, at a cubit from the ground. Her lips were painted, her eyebrows were deep black, and the eyes themselves almost terrifying. There were beads of moisture on her forehead like a vapour on white marble. She did not speak, but she and Herod looked at one another.

A snap of fingers was heard in the balcony. She went up there, came down again, and then brought out these words with a childish air, lisping a little:

"I want you to give me, in a dish, the head . . ." She had forgotten the name, but began again, smiling: "The head of Iaokanan!"

The Tetrarch sank back in a heap, overwhelmed.

He was bound by his word, and the people were waiting. And then another thought passed through his mind. What of that death which had been predicted to him? If it were passed on to another his own might be averted. Supposing Iaokanan were really Elias, he would be able to escape it; and if he were not, the murder ceased to matter.

Mannæï was by his side and grasped his intention. Vitellius called the man back as he was going out and gave him the password for the sentinels on guard round the pit.

That was a relief! A moment, and all would be over.

Mannæï, however, was not very quick at his work. He came back, but in a state of collapse.

For forty years he had practised as an executioner. It was he who had drowned Aristobulus, strangled Alexander, burned Matathias alive, beheaded Zosimus, Pappus, Joseph, and

Antipater—and he did not dare to kill Iaokanan! His teeth chattered, and he was shak-
ing all over.

He had seen the Great Angel of the Samaritans in front of the pit, covered all over with
eyes and brandishing a huge sword, red and
jagged like a flame. Two soldiers whom he
brought as witnesses would say as much; or
so he thought.

But they had, in fact, seen nothing, except
a Jewish officer who had rushed on them and
was now no more.

Herodias let loose her fury in a coarse and
biting stream of insults. She tore her finger-
nails on the grille of the balcony, and the two
carved lions seemed to be gnawing her shoulders and roaring like her.

Antipas followed her lead, as did the priests,
Pharisees, and soldiers, one and all demanding
their revenge, while the rest of the company were indignant at having their pleasure
postponed.

Mannæï went out hiding his face.

The guests found the interval even longer
than it was the first time; they were getting
bored.

Suddenly a noise of footsteps echoed in the
corridors. The suspense became unbearable.

The head came in—Mannæï holding it by the hair at arm's length, proud of the applause which greeted him. He put it on a dish and then offered it to Salome. She went nimbly up into the balcony; and a few minutes later the head was brought back by the old woman whom the Tetrarch had noticed on a house-roof in the morning, and seen later in the chamber of Herodias.

He drew back to avoid seeing the head. Vitellius gave it an unconcerned look.

Mannæï left the dais and showed it to the Roman officers, and then to all the diners sitting on that side. They examined it. The sharp edge of his implement had slanted down and cut into the jaw. The corners of the mouth were convulsively drawn. There was blood, already clotted, sprinkled in the beard. The closed eyes were as pale as shells, and rays from the candles which stood round caught them.

The head reached the table of the priests. One of the Pharisees turned it over curiously; then Mannæï set it upright again and placed it before Aulus, whom it awakened. The drowsed eyes of the one and the dead eyes of the other seemed to say a word to each other through their parted lashes.

Then Mannæï presented it to Antipas. Tears flowed down the Tetrarch's cheeks. The torches went out, the guests departed; and in the banqueting hall there was now only Antipas, still gazing on the severed head with his hands pressed against his temples, while Phanuel stood in the middle of the great nave and prayed in a murmur, with his arms stretched out.

.   .   .   .   .   .

At the moment when the sun rose two men who had been sent out by Iaokanan came in with their long-expected answer.

They confided it to Phanuel, who went into a rapture. Then he showed them the lamentable object on the dish, among the remnants of the feast. One of the men said to him:

"Take courage! He has gone down to the dead to proclaim the Christ!"

The Essene now understood the meaning of those words, "I must decrease that He may increase."

And all three of them took the head of Iaokanan and went away towards Galilee. As it was very heavy, they carried it alternately.

THE END